THE ODDS AGAINST CIRCLE L

THE ODDS AGAINST CIRCLE L

Lewis B. Patten

First published in Great Britain by Chivers Gunsmoke.
First published in the United States by Ace Books

Published in Large Print 2006 by ISIS Publishing Ltd.,
7 Centremead, Osney Mead, Oxford OX2 0ES
United Kingdom
by arrangement with
Golden West Literary Agency

British Library Cataloguing in Publication Data
Patten, Lewis B.
The odds against Circle L. – Large print ed. –
(Sagebrush western series)
1. Western stories
2. Large type books
I. Title
813.5'4 [F]

ISBN–10 0–7531–7558–4 (hb)
ISBN–13 978–0–7531–7558–3 (hb)

Printed and bound in Great Britain by
T. J. International Ltd., Padstow, Cornwall

CHAPTER ONE

Taggart Landry reined his horse to a halt at the top of the long rise looking northward toward the town. Frowning, he stared down at it, and suddenly it was as though he had never even been away. Scattered almost untidily along the bank of Cheyenne Creek, the town dozed in the mid-morning sun exactly as he remembered it. A few horses drowsed at the hitch rails in front of the saloons. The white church steeple still needed paint. The schoolyard was still bare from many running, scuffing feet. Three or four swaybacked horses still stood patiently beneath the lean-to out back. He thought wryly, "Hell, it hasn't changed a bit."

He touched his horse's sides with his heels and the animal moved ahead, entering the road halfway down the rise. Taggart kept him in the road after that, stopping once more to briefly eye the sign standing at the edge of town. It read simply, "Landry, Wyoming. Pop. 154"

He realized that he was approaching this with something very close to dread, or fear: fear that his father was dead. Or worse, that he would not welcome his son, who had now come home.

He also realized that his own feelings had not changed. The things that had made him leave home still remained. Why, then, had he come back?

Out of respect, he supposed. Out of affection too, affection which had not, unfortunately, been returned. But there was another reason why he had come back. He needed ties with his family. Everyone needed ties. He needed to belong someplace. He particularly needed to belong now that he had glimpsed the way a man can drift when he is accountable to no one but himself.

Landry, Wyoming — the town was named for his father, either dead or near to death if Lew Wintergill's letter was to be believed.

Landry, Wyoming, an island in vast, sprawling Circle L ranch, which Emmett Landry had taken and held by force, against the Cheyennes, to whom it had once belonged and against the settlers, who would plow it and put it into crops.

Suddenly Taggart went on, hurrying. He had to know and he had to know right now. He had to know if old Emmett Landry was still alive.

His horse trotted steadily along the street, at this end lined with residences. Close to the edge of town were the homes of the more solid citizens, the banker, the feed store operator, the mercantile store owner, the town's lawyer and its judge. Closer to the center of town lived those less eminent, the saloonkeepers, the livery barn operator, a few cattle traders, the gunsmith and the owner of the lumber yard. Beyond these houses were the businesses of the town, lining both sides of

Main Street all the way to the bridge across Cheyenne Creek.

Halfway to the bridge Taggart could see the sheriff's office and jail, a stone block building, square as the stones of which it was built and flat-roofed.

Dun-colored it stood, blending with the land, symbolic of the violence of the land, of the violence of the men who inhabited it. Taggart kept his glance straight ahead, not wanting to talk to anyone until he first had talked to Lew Wintergill.

He halted his horse at the hitch rail before the jail and swung stiffly down. He looped the reins around the rail, then pushed his hat back on his head and stared at the barred windows of the jail.

He was a tall young man, twenty-four on his last birthday. Lean and rawboned, he carried no extra weight. His face was almost gaunt, and dark from exposure to the elements. His eyes were blue, and sharp, but without the authority of his father's eyes. He was a man looking aimlessly around, who had not yet fixed his glance upon a goal. But there was something else in his face as he stood before the sheriff's office here in his own home town. It was a thing too obscure for the average man to recognize but a thing any good lawman would know instantly. Taggart Landry was wary of the law. For some reason, Taggart Landry was afraid.

Determinedly, almost, he stepped across the boardwalk and opened the door to the sheriff's office. He stepped inside.

Even the smell was familiar here, he thought. It was the smell of disinfectant, used in the jail at the rear, the smell of stale pipe smoke and the smell of coffee, simmering in a pot on the heating stove. He stared across the room at the sheriff, sitting with his feet on his littered, roll-top desk.

The feet came down and the swivel chair creaked as the sheriff got to his feet. He said harshly, "Well I'll be damned! The letter found you after all!"

He crossed to Taggart and stuck out his hand. "Glad to see you, Tag."

Taggart took the hand, short-fingered but calloused and powerful. He said, "Hello, Mr. Wintergill. How's pa? Is he . . . ?"

"He ain't dead, boy. I won't say he's all right because he ain't. He's still alive — I reckon waitin' for you to come."

Taggart shook his head. "Waiting for something, maybe, but not for me."

Wintergill did not reply. He studied Taggart until the penetrating quality of his stare made Taggart look away. Taggart crossed to the window and stared outside, angry with himself because he had failed to meet the sheriff's glance. He said, "Is he out at the ranch?"

"Yup. You know him, boy. Even if he knew he was dyin', he wouldn't come to town."

"Doesn't he know?" Taggart swung his head, determined to meet the sheriff's glance this time.

Wintergill's eyes were blue-gray, hard and impersonal as bullets looking out the cylinder of a gun. Taggart forced himself to hold the sheriff's glance and managed it. Wintergill shook his head. "I don't know whether he does or not. Your brother Miles had a doctor come all the way from Cheyenne, but I don't know what they told your pa."

"What did they tell you?"

"That his heart failed. Or damn near did."

"And that he was going to die?"

"Might. Not would."

"Why didn't Miles write me? Why'd he get you to do it for him?"

"He didn't get me to, son. I did it on my own. The old man wasn't in no shape to write anyone at first and I knew Miles wouldn't write to you. I'd found one of your letters in the old man's pocket the day he collapsed out there on the street, so I just took it on myself. I figured he'd want you to know."

Taggart turned his head and stared out of the window again. He wondered how his letter had happened to be in the old man's pocket. Probably he'd just stuck it there absent-mindedly and forgot to take it out again.

He asked, "Is he still in bed?"

Wintergill shook his head. "Nope. He's up and dressed every day. Sits in a chair on the porch. He ain't much better, but I guess he ain't gettin' worse." The sheriff's voice thinned emphatically. "Like I said before, I figure he's just waitin' for you to come home."

Taggart swung around and stuck out his hand. "Thanks, Mr. Wintergill. Thanks for writing me."

Wintergill took the hand, gripping hard and then releasing it. Staring straight at Taggart's face he said, "I like that old man, Tag. He's a lot of man. I'd do damn near anything for him."

Taggart suddenly had to get away. He mumbled, "Thanks again, Mr. Wintergill," turned and hurried to the door. He yanked it open and plunged outside.

On the boardwalk, he forced himself to halt, fighting his almost overpowering compulsion to run. It was as though he could feel the sheriff's eyes on his back, burning where they touched.

He clenched his fists at his sides, hesitating between vaulting to his horse's back and galloping out of town and waiting a while to make his departure look deliberate. He decided on the latter, turned and hurried downstreet toward the nearest saloon.

It was the Buckhorn. He batted the doors open and went inside. He went straight to the bar without even looking around the room.

Sam Leonard, bartender for Blossom Shane, who owned the place, came down the bar to him, wiping his hairy-backed hands on his apron. "Tag! When'd you git back to town?"

"Few minutes ago. Gimme a beer."

"Sure Tag. On the house." He drew a beer, raked the head off with a stick and brought it down to Tag. "Too bad about your pa. You been out to the ranch to see him yet?"

Taggart shook his head. He raised the mug and took a long drink. He put it down, wiping his mouth with the back of his hand. That was when he saw Leach out of the corner of his eye.

Or at least he thought it was Leach sitting over there at a table watching him. Suddenly there was a cold spot in his chest and his knees felt weak.

He let his hand slide toward the edge of the bar. He could yank out his gun, whirl and fire and kill Leach right here and now. But how would he explain it afterward?

Deliberately, slowly, making it look casual, he turned his body until he could look at Leach. His eyes met Leach's with an impact that was almost physical.

There was a coldly sardonic expression on Leach's face. His eyes mocked Taggart in the instant before they slid away without acknowledging that he knew Taggart recognized him. Leach poured himself another drink from the bottle in front of him. He did not look up again.

Taggart turned back to the bar. He gulped the beer and slid the glass down the bar to Sam. "Fill it up, Sam." His voice was harsh and curt enough to make Sam look at him curiously.

Holding his clenched hands beneath the bar, Tag fought to control himself. He might have known this would be inevitable, that someday he'd run into Leach or one of the others somewhere. But why did it have to be here? Why did it have to be now?

Sam brought him his second beer and he paid for it absently. He sipped it, feeling Leach watching him the way he had felt the sheriff watching him earlier. He'd only been gone two years but a lot had happened in those two short years. A lot had happened he wished hadn't happened at all.

Scowling, he stared at the beer in front of him. He'd been angry when he left here two years ago. He'd been mad clear through. Now, looking back, he could see that his anger had been childish. So had the things his anger made him do.

But it was too late to change anything. What had happened had happened and he'd have to live with it. Killing Leach wouldn't hide what he had done. Besides, it was doubtful if he could kill Leach. Leach was almost incredibly fast with that gun of his and he'd be expecting something of the sort from Tag.

He finished his beer. He made himself grin at Sam Leonard. "Thanks for the beer, Sam. See you some other time."

"Sure Tag. Tell the old man hello for me."

Taggart nodded. He hurried from the saloon without looking at Leach. Maybe Leach was just passing through, he told himself. Maybe he'd never see Leach again after today. But he didn't believe it. He didn't believe it at all. In his mind he could still see the sardonic, mocking expression in Leach's eyes. He'd be able to see that for a long, long time.

The doors swung shut behind Taggart Landry. For a moment they continued to swing idly back and forth.

Leach got up from the table. He picked up his bottle and carried it to the bar. He put it down. "Get a couple of glasses, bartender. Have a drink with me."

Sam Leonard got two glasses and put them down in front of Leach. Leach poured them full.

He was a thickset man, in his late thirties. A careful, wary man. A man who reminded people who saw him of an animal, a hungry, predatory animal. His eyes were gray and as cold as a winter wind. His mouth had a cynical, mocking twist to it. His whiskers were dark brown, unshaven for about three days. He wore a sweeping brown mustache that he kept stroking with his hand. He said, "That young fella looked familiar someway. I been tryin' to place him. Seems like I've seen him someplace before."

Leonard gulped his drink, exhaled noisily, then wiped his mouth with the back of his hand. "You could have, I guess. He's been gone a couple of years but I don't know where he's been."

"What's his name? Maybe it'll make me remember. A thing like this bothers a man. I'll be puzzlin' about it until I remember him."

"Taggart Landry. His name's Tag Landry."

"Ain't Landry the name of this town?"

"Yup. Named for his Pa. The old man hacked a ranch out of Cheyenne country in the early days. Biggest ranch for a couple hundred miles, I guess. It surrounds the town. No matter where you go from here, you're on Circle L."

Leach said, "Hmmm." He raised his eyes to Sam. "Have another one, friend?"

"Well thanks." Leonard poured himself a second drink.

Leach said, "He don't look like he came from a wealthy family."

"Well he does." Leonard's face was slightly flushed. "His old man's got thirty-forty thousand cattle out there on that ranch an' everything's free an' clear. Tag had a fallin' out with the old man, though. That's why he went away."

"How come he's back?"

"The old man's sick. There's been some talk that he might just up an' die."

"And that would leave young Taggart owning that great big ranch?" There was a certain excitement in Leach's voice but Leonard didn't notice it. He was eyeing Leach's bottle and turning his empty glass around and around. He said, "Huh uh. Not all of it. Tag has got another brother, Miles."

Leach glanced at Leonard, then poured him another drink. Leonard gulped it down. A woman entered the saloon through a rear door. She looked at Leonard and at Leach.

She was a middle-aged woman and overweight. Her low-cut blue silk dress showed an enormous expanse of huge white shoulders, of swelling breasts beneath. Her face was painted and hard, her voice both husky and harsh. She said, "Sam!"

Sam looked around, guiltily wiping his mouth. "I only had a couple, Blossom. A man ought to be sociable."

Leach said, "I asked him, ma'am. It's my fault, I guess."

She put her small, hard eyes on him. She eyed him up and down, missing nothing. There was no softening in her eyes and she did not speak.

Leach looked away first. He grinned faintly at Leonard. "I got a feeling I've wore my welcome out." He pushed himself away from the bar and headed toward the doors. He banged out through them, pausing just outside to bite the end off a cigar and light it up. Puffing luxuriously, he stared upstreet, then down, at the vast expanse of land lying beyond the town. He had a feeling he was onto something that could mean a lot to him; he felt like a man who has just found gold.

Decisively, he headed for the telegraph station. He couldn't handle this alone, and he wasn't fool enough to try.

CHAPTER TWO

Riding out toward home, Tag was remembering a lot of things he had been trying not to think about of late. Things like his bitterness toward his father a couple of years ago when he first went away. He'd been hurt and he'd wanted to hurt back. Doing so took the form of thinking, in the back of his mind at least, that it would serve the old man right if one of his sons became notorious.

He'd had a little money and there had been no immediate urgency about going to work. He'd made friends with a bunch of men, of whom Leach was one, in a saloon down in Indian Territory.

One thing led inevitably to another. At first he just drank with the men, and played cards with them. But eventually they ran out of money and so did Tag.

Five of them, Leach, Tag, Romolo, Sierra and Quinlan, who assumed the position of leader, rode north into Kansas and held up a bank. They had the drop on everybody, but one of the guards had to try and make a hero out of himself. Quinlan shot him, and the five seized the loot and rode away, leaving the guard lying face down just inside the door.

Quinlan had planned it so that they robbed the bank in late afternoon. By the time a posse got organized, it was almost dark. The posse had to give up trailing and wait for daylight but the five suffered no such handicap. They rode all night, and the next day split up, each man hiding his own trail from the pursuit. They got clean away.

They planned to get together again down in Indian Territory, where they were to split up the loot, which Quinlan had carried because he was the only one they all trusted. But Tag never went back to Indian Territory and he never shared in the loot. He only shared the guilt. It had been months before he stopped seeing, in his uneasy dreams, the guard crumpling forward and afterward lying still as death on the white tile floor of the little bank.

One thing Tag surely knew. He wanted no part of an outlaw's life. He wanted no part of running, and hiding, and forever looking over your shoulder to see if someone was following you. Loafing around the saloons with Quinlan and Leach and the others had been all right for a while. But not after the guard was shot. Not after the robbery.

He kicked his horse into a steady, bone-jolting trot. What was Leach doing in Landry anyway? Had seeing him been pure chance, or had Leach known who Taggart Landry was? His scowl deepened suddenly. It didn't matter whether Leach had known before or not. The important thing was that he knew now. And Tag was sure he'd take full advantage of the knowledge to profit himself and his friends. He should have picked a fight with Leach and killed him if he could, he thought. He was going to be sorry he had not.

Thinking about that, he realized he couldn't have done it, even if his life had depended on it. He couldn't take it upon himself to decide that a man should die and then cold-bloodedly execute him. That was what it would have amounted to, despite the risk that he would be killed himself.

The land was rolling here, a well-remembered land in which each landmark was as familiar as an old, old friend. Coming back should have warmed him but it did not. An icy chill was growing in his spine, because he knew he was going to have to pay for his involvement in that Kansas bank robbery two years ago. The law said he was as guilty of murder in the guard's death as Quinlan, because he had been helping to commit a felony.

He shook his head angrily, fixing his glance on the horizon ahead where he knew the home place was. He was borrowing trouble for himself. He hadn't spoken to Leach and Leach hadn't spoken to him. Why should Leach want to make trouble for him? By his failure to show up and claim his share of the loot, he had only made more available to the other four. Besides, what could Leach do? He couldn't turn him over to the law without also involving himself.

The sun climbed steadily to its zenith overhead, then began its slow descent toward the horizon in the west. The dusty miles fell away behind the hoofs of Taggart's horse.

It was late afternoon when he glimpsed the buildings of the home place. The sun's rays had turned orange, and were slanting sharply across the land, throwing elongated shadows from every building and every tree.

Staring at this place that had been home to him all his life, Taggart felt his chest tighten with something that was close to pain. He should never have gone away. His jealousy of Miles had been childish. There was room enough here for both of them. There was room too in the old man's heart for both his sons. Miles was the eldest; it was natural for him to also be the favorite.

He would stay here now. He'd work and would make his father proud of him. Perhaps he could repay what the old man had given him by taking the load off him now that he was old and sick. But in spite of his joy at being home again, in spite of his determination to make up for the past, the coldness lingered in his chest. The memory of Leach lingered in his mind.

He knew, as he nudged his horse into motion again, that it was not going to be easy for him. Eventually, no matter what Leach did or didn't do, he was going to have to pay for his part in that bank robbery and killing in Kansas two years ago.

Narrowing his eyes against the glare of the sinking sun, he stared at the scattered, sprawling buildings ahead of him. There was the house, tall and gaunt, a two-storied house that had stood like a sentinel on the Wyoming plain for longer than Taggart had been alive. There was the barn, three times the size of the house and built solidly of logs hauled from fifty miles away. There were half a score of other, smaller buildings: the bunkhouse, the ice house, a chicken house, a couple of storage sheds. There were the two windmills, spinning briskly in the wind. There were the corrals, holding a dozen or more horses at this time of day. There was the haying machinery and beyond the barn were the remains of the haystacks put up last year.

Smoke rose from the kitchen chimney of the house, from the tin chimney of the cookshack which was part of the bunkhouse. A man walked across the yard to the hand pump and worked its handle vigorously.

Suddenly, movement coming from his right caught Taggart's eye. He saw a solitary rider approaching him and narrowed his eyes against the glare, staring, trying to recognize the man.

There was something familiar about him, even at a distance of a quarter mile. Something about the man's bearing perhaps, something about the way he sat on his horse. Suddenly Taggart knew who he was. The rider was his brother.

He reined his horse aside on a course that would intercept Miles just short of the house. He lightly raked his horse's sides, enough to lift him to a lope.

While he was still several hundred yards away, Miles apparently recognized him, for he brought his horse to a sudden halt. He stared at Tag. It was too far to see his brother's face, to make out the expression it wore. But his body, the positions of both his head and shoulders were eloquent. There was plain hostility in the way he sat, in the way his head thrust itself forward toward Tag. And when Tag got close enough, he saw the same hostility in Miles's angry eyes, in the set of his wide, thin mouth.

Miles was five years older than Tag. He bore the same name as Tag, but there the resemblance ended. Miles was big, with shoulders like a bull. His neck was thick, usually thrust forward aggressively. His eyes were blue and set wide apart above a nose broken and flattened years before by a horse's kick.

Tag said, "Hello Miles."

Miles did not acknowledge the greeting. He just stared at Tag coldly, with plain dislike. Tag felt his temper stir. Damn Miles anyway! Who the hell did he think he was, sitting there glaring as though Tag had no right to even be here on this land?

Determinedly, he beat the stirring temper down. He wasn't going to make up for the past if he fought with Miles the minute he got home. He said, "I heard Pa was sick. I came right away. How is he, Miles?"

"A lot you care. You been gone two years and I doubt you've written twice in all that time. Maybe you thought he'd already be dead and you could claim half the ranch."

"But he isn't dead. That's what you're saying, isn't it?"

"He ain't dead. He ain't well, neither, and seein' you won't help him get well. You got a nerve coming home after all these years."

"Two years is all." Taggart wanted to lash back at Miles but he forced his voice to be mild, forced his eyes to regard Miles without anger but only with irritation. He said, "You and I have never exactly gotten along, but I don't want to fight with you. Especially now. I belong here on this ranch, just the same as you."

"The hell you do! You didn't care enough to stay and help work the place. It's mine, now, all of it."

"Is that what Pa says, Miles?"

"It don't make no difference what he says. Not any more. He ain't himself. He ain't the man he was when you went away. I'm running Circle L, not him."

"Does he know that?"

"He knows it. You're damned right he knows it. And you'd better know it too."

"I'm going to see him, Miles. Then I'll decide whether I'll stay or go."

"Huh uh. I've already decided that. You go." Miles swung ponderously from his horse. He moved away from the animal and stood there, legs spread, eyes smoldering, an ugly look on his mouth.

Taggart shrugged resignedly. "All right Miles. If that's the way it's got to be." He got down from his horse. He unbuckled his gun belt, then hung it on the saddle horn. He walked toward Miles warily, glancing once toward the buildings to see if they were being observed. The sheriff had said his father spent the days sitting on the porch, which wasn't visible from here. At least his father wouldn't have to watch his two sons fight the way they would fight today.

This wasn't the first time Tag had fought Miles. He'd fought him twenty or thirty times, he supposed. At first, when they'd both been small, the outcome had always been cut and dry, always the same. Miles was bigger than he, and stronger too. Miles whipped him every time they fought.

But later — after he'd gotten most of his growth — he began to come out better in his fights with Miles. He began to inflict punishment where previously he had only taken it. He began to feel that eventually it would be possible for him to win.

The fights became less frequent as Miles apparently sensed the same possibility. But he never had really beaten Miles even though he'd come close to it just before he left. Now he was going to find out if he could beat Miles and at the same time he was going to find out if he could stay here at Circle L. If he couldn't whip Miles, he couldn't stay. It was as simple as that.

He was still twenty feet away when Miles suddenly rushed at him. He sidestepped, too late. Miles's shoulder struck him in the chest and the impact was like the savage kick of a half-broke mule. He felt the air gust out of him, felt himself falling and felt the impact as he struck the ground flat on his back.

Miles's momentum carried him on beyond, but he failed to keep his feet. He sprawled on the ground, rolling immediately and coming ponderously up again.

Tag, too, was getting up. The pain in his chest was terrible and he gasped frantically for breath, wincing with pain each time he filled his lungs and exhaled. Another blow like that and he'd be out of the fight, finished, beaten. He had to stay away from Miles until his strength returned.

Miles rushed a second time, swinging his right fist in a wild, crazy, roundhouse swing that might have broken

Tag's neck if it had connected solidly. It did not. Tag leaped to one side, ducked and avoided it, and again the uncontrolled momentum of the rush carried Miles on past. This time he did not fall but turned, head lowered, glowering and panting like a bull.

He began to curse his brother, with savage bitterness. He advanced slowly, apparently through rushing and determined to play a more careful game. Tag backed as Miles advanced, still fighting for breath, still weak in the knees, still light of head. He couldn't retreat forever but he had no other choice right now.

He had never seen so much bitterness in Miles. It startled him to see it, but he knew it must have been there all the time. It was not a thing born today, in the last few minutes since he'd encountered Miles. It had to have been in Miles for years. Maybe it had always been present, but carefully hidden so that no one had ever realized it was there.

Tag backed into one of the horses. Believing Tag was trapped, Miles rushed again, abandoning caution and carefulness. Tag sidestepped him swiftly, sensing the movement of the horse dancing away in fright. Unthinkingly, he stuck out a foot and tripped Miles as his brother charged past.

Miles sprawled forward, straight into the horse, still trying desperately to get out of the way. The horse's eyes showed their whites as they rolled toward this man who had blundered into him. Thoroughly frightened, the horse lashed out with one hind foot. The hoof caught Miles on the top of the head, stunned him and left him flat on his back. Tag closed in and stood over him, staring down.

Nothing had been settled here today. The settlement had just been postponed. He'd have to fight Miles sooner or later and when he did . . . An appalling certainty came over him. When Miles and he did fight, only one of them would emerge from the fight alive. He was sure of that, terrible as it was to think of brother killing brother to survive.

Sanity began to return to Miles's eyes but he didn't move. He stared up at Tag with smoldering, bitter, terrible hate, hate that made Tag feel cold. Tag said, "It will have to wait, Miles. It will have to wait."

Miles did not reply and Tag wasn't even sure he could. He stared down at Miles for a moment more, then turned away and walked to his horse. He picked up the reins and swung to the horse's back. He turned the animal toward the house. He did not look back.

No longer was there joy in coming home, in the familiar things he remembered, in the memories that came crowding into his mind. Over all his thoughts hung a gloomy cloud, a premonition of disaster, of impending destruction for them all.

Miles was demented — out of his mind. There was little doubt of that. But Miles was a reality, just as this ranch was, just as their ailing father was. And realities could not be changed.

He approached the house reluctantly. He rounded the corner of it and suddenly saw his father sitting in the cane rocker on the porch.

CHAPTER THREE

It was a different Emmett Landry that Tag saw sitting on the porch. He remembered a big man, of bony ruggedness — a man to stand spread-legged on this land and defy it to destroy him.

He had stood thus, hurling defiance at the land for as long as Tag could remember. He had met its force and violence with his own force and violence and he had tamed it to his will. He had stood like a rock against the yelling, galloping hordes of Indians. He had stood against the howling blizzards that came horizontally out of the north, freezing everything in their paths. He had stood against the summer heat and the drought, and the ponderous, crawling, persistent wagons of the settlers, who, if he had not prevented them, would have plowed this land and put it in crops, crops that could not come up because there was never enough rain. The only things that could survive were the tough grass plants and other things that were indigenous. The grass and the prairie animals and Emmett Landry and Emmett Landry's cattle. These were the only things that could survive.

The settlers had gone, and the Indians were gone, but the land and its violence remained. And now

Emmett Landry had changed from the strong, bony man with the craggy, bony face and the ice-blue eyes, to a broken, sick, helpless man rocking his life away on the creaking floor boards of the front porch here.

Tag halted his horse and sat looking at his father, meeting the old man's eyes. There was pity in him, but he would not show it because he knew it would finish the destruction illness had already begun. Instead he grinned, a genuine grin because he was genuinely glad, that he had at last come home.

He got down from his horse, leaving the reins trailing, and walked to the porch and climbed the steps. He said, "Hello Pa," and stood like a tongue-tied kid the way he had so many times before.

Emmett Landry's voice was a hoarse croak and Tag realized it was probably the first time he had spoken for several hours. He said a single word, "Tag!" and his eyes brightened with unshed tears.

Tag crossed to him and sat down facing him on the front porch rail. Awkwardly he stuck out a hand and the old man raised his own frail hand and took it tremblingly. The hand, bony and thin, without flesh or warmth, clung to Tag's with an almost feverish strength and there was something in old Emmett Landry's eyes . . . something that could not be misunderstood.

Tag knew he had been wrong. For all these years he had been wrong. He had not been slighted in his father's affections; he was his father's favorite. It had only seemed that Miles was because the old man had bent over backward trying to be fair.

The sudden realization flooded Tag with warmth. He grinned at his father foolishly, his own eyes brightening with tears. But the smile faded suddenly when he thought of Miles. He may have been blind and stupid, but he guessed Miles had always known. It explained Miles's almost fanatical hatred of him. It explained a great many things.

He said, "The sheriff wrote me and said that you were sick. I came as soon as I got his letter."

Emmett Landry raised a hand and brushed almost angrily at his eyes. He said hoarsely, "I'll be all right now that you've come home. I'll be up and around in no time. Right now, by God, I want a drink to celebrate."

"Sure. I'll get it and bring it out."

He went into the house. It was just as he remembered it. It even smelled the same, a little dusty, a little leathery — a lived-in, pleasant smell. He went to the cupboard where the whiskey was kept and got a bottle out. He went to the kitchen and got a couple of glasses. He carried them out to the porch, poured a glass half full and handed it to his father. He filled his own and raised it to his mouth, looking silently at his father over the rim.

There was more color in his father's face than there had been before. There was more sparkle in his eyes. The sheriff had been wrong. Emmett Landry had not been waiting for his youngest son to come home so that he could die. He had been waiting for Tag to come so he could get well.

Fiercely he tried to convince himself that this was true. The old man gulped the whiskey, coughed a couple of times, grinned weakly at Tag. Tag thought, *He's got to get well! He's got to!* But he could not close his eyes to the weakness apparent in his father's fleshless frame. And he knew that anything, any sudden shock, could cause his father's death.

Any shock . . . Like seeing his two sons locked in mortal combat, like knowing his youngest son was a murderer and a thief in the eyes of the law. The mending of Emmett Landry's heart and body was going to take a lot of time. And it was up to Taggart to see that he got that time.

Out of the corner of his eye he saw Miles ride in. The old man glanced up, then glanced back at Tag again. He said, "Time to go in, I guess." He waited, as though for Tag to help him up.

Tag didn't offer to. He waited until his father was up, then walked with him into the house. He said, "I'll go put up my horse."

The old man turned his head. "You're going to stay?"

Taggart hesitated. He didn't know whether he was going to stay or not. Even if he wanted to, he wasn't sure staying was best for anyone. Miles would resent his presence here. Miles had forced him into a fight once and would again. This conflict between his sons certainly wasn't going to help the old man improve.

Emmett Landry said, "Tag! This is your home. This is where you belong."

Tag turned his head and stared into his father's eyes. The light was not as strong in here as it had been outside but there was no mistaking the expression on Emmett Landry's face. Almost reluctantly Tag nodded his head. "I'll stay, Pa. At least for now."

The old man slumped with relief. He reached out a hand and it closed over Tag's shoulder. There was surprising strength in the grip of that hand. It squeezed and fell away.

Tag grinned at him. His father returned the grin, more strongly now, and said. "Go put up your horse. Tonight we'll talk. I want to know everything you've done since you've been away."

Tag nodded and went back outside. His face was sombre as he remembered one thing he had done since going away that he would never tell. And he couldn't help remembering seeing Leach in town.

Two things he must do if he was going to stay. He must avoid open conflict with Miles and he must keep secret his participation in the Kansas bank robbery. Frowning, he led his horse to the barn.

There was a little knot of men in front of the great, sliding doors. All of them were watching him. Miles was there, an open challenge in his eyes. Cass Borden was also there, Cass who had been foreman of Circle L since Taggart was a little boy. He grinned at Cass, but the grin faded when he saw the expression on Cass's face.

He stopped half a dozen feet away from the group. He didn't look at Miles, only at Cass as he said, "You too? Maybe I ought to have stayed away."

Cass was leathery, of medium height but broad of shoulder and hand and face. His eyes were gray, unruffled and competent. He said in his gravely voice, "Maybe you should have Tag, maybe you should have. Why the hell did you come back anyway?"

Irritation touched Taggart's mind. His mouth thinned with it. "Couple of reasons I guess. The sheriff wrote and said the old man was sick. I guess that's why I came." He scowled at Cass. "But I'll tell you why I'm going to stay." He switched his glance to Miles. "I'm going to stay because this is home. It's home to me just as much as it's home to any of you. Maybe more."

"And because you figure you've got something coming if the old man dies?"

Tag stared at Cass angrily. "I never even thought of that angle until Miles brought it up. But even if I had, what's wrong with it? If he didn't want me to have anything, he'd cut me out of his will. Maybe he's done just that for all I know. I haven't asked and I don't intend to ask. Miles is the one who's worrying about who's going to get Circle L."

He pushed past the group and led his horse into the barn. Here too it was familiar and unchanged, even to the smell of hay and dry manure, of leather and horses and grain. He put his saddle and blanket in the tackroom, then led his horse to a stall. He gave him a can of oats and a couple of forks of hay. He returned to the tackroom and flung his bridle down where his saddle was.

He stood there for a moment, staring at the little group that was now beginning to disperse. Miles came into the barn, leading his horse, scowling at his brother as he went by. Cass went across the yard to the pump and began to wash up. A couple of the others accompanied him. The rest disappeared, some going to the bunkhouse, some coming into the barn to put their saddles away.

Most of them were new, hands Tag didn't know, but that wasn't too surprising, he guessed. He had been gone two years and cowhands were a fiddlefooted lot, rarely staying in one place long.

He went outside, stopped and stared at Cass for a long time. He wished that Cass had understood. He wished that Cass had welcomed him. Shrugging, he crossed the yard to the pump. A couple of cowhands stared at him curiously, appraisingly, as he approached. He worked the pumphandle until a stream of water gushed out. He stuck his head under the spout, groped for the soap and lathered his hands and face. He rinsed off and reached for the flour-sack towel.

The two cowhands were gone. He dried himself, hung up the towel and headed for the house, frowning lightly as he walked. Talk of his father's death, of inheritance, had disturbed and upset him. Circle L was home to him, not an inheritance. He went into the kitchen.

Wong, the Chinese cook, turned his head, grinned a wide welcome at him. "Mistuh Tag. Glad to see you come. Now old man get well quick."

Tag grinned warmly back. The old man had welcomed him. Now Wong had too.

But a lot of questions remained unanswered in his mind. Why the hostility on the part of Miles and Cass? Above all, why should his own brother hate him the way Miles hated him? There had to be more to it than resentment because he had guessed the old man favored Tag.

He sat down and accepted the cup of coffee Wong brought to him. Questions continued to torment his mind. What had Leach been doing in town? Why hadn't Leach spoken to him? He was sure the man had recognized him. He was sure of that.

Uneasiness began to grow in his troubled mind. He'd see Leach again. He was sure he would. And the trouble with his brother Miles was far from settled yet. Maybe he ought to go away again. Maybe staying would only bring trouble for everyone, including the old man who certainly didn't need any more trouble than he already had.

He shook his head almost imperceptibly. Going away wouldn't solve anything — not for his father — not for himself. His father was ill, desperately so. He had become ill while Tag was gone, had worsened and weakened while Tag was gone. If he left again, his father would die. That was a certainty.

But if he stayed — there would be trouble, and conflict, and perhaps even death. He could feel that, could sense it like a premonition. His father might die anyway. He might be driven to death by the things that would happen here.

He finished the last of the scalding coffee. He'd stay for a while, he decided finally. He'd stay for a little while. He could always leave if the conflict between himself and Miles became too deadly serious. He could always leave if Leach showed up, before Leach turned him over to the law or told his father what he had done. In the meantime, he'd do the best he could to get along with everyone, with Miles and with Cass as well. Once his decision was made, it was easier. His mind relaxed and stopped tormenting him.

Miles came banging into the kitchen, crossed it and disappeared into the living room. Cass came in, got a cup from the cupboard and filled it with coffee at the stove. He crossed the room and sat down at the table across from Tag.

Tag said, "I'm going to stay."

Cass shrugged but he did not reply.

Tag said, "I'm going to stay for a while at least. Pa wants me to stay."

"You don't have to explain yourself to me."

Tag scowled at him. "Maybe not. Maybe I don't." Anger made him feel reckless. It wouldn't matter with Cass. But with Miles . . .

He said, "You've been here since I was just a little kid. Half of what I know I learned from you. Why don't you want me here?"

Cass stared at him a moment, then looked away almost guiltily. He said quietly, "It ain't that I don't want you here. It's just that you're bringing trouble home with you and trouble is one thing the old man doesn't need."

"What do you mean, I'm bringing trouble home with me?"

Cass frowned as his eyes studied Tag. "Trouble with Miles, I guess. It's partly that. But there's something else . . ."

"What do you mean, something else?"

Cass stared steadily into Tag's eyes. He stared so long and so hard that Tag had to look away. It was as though Cass was able to look straight into his soul and read everything hidden there.

Cass said softly, "That. That's what I mean. Whatever it is that makes it impossible for you to look straight at me. Something's happened to you since you've been away, something you're ashamed of and don't want known. I don't intend to let you drag it back here with you. The old man's got all the trouble he can handle as it is."

Tag felt a surge of anger at Cass for ferreting out his secret even if he didn't know exactly what it was and at himself for betraying it by his failure to meet Cass's eyes.

He stared across the table at Cass, and this time his eyes were unwavering. He said, "I won't let anything hurt him. That's a solemn promise, Cass."

Cass said noncommittally, "Promises are hard to keep. They're easy to make but damned hard to keep."

"I'll keep this one. I'll keep it or I'll go away."

Cass studied him critically for a long, long time. At last he nodded grudgingly, and shrugged. "I guess that's good enough. I guess it'll have to be good enough. For now at least."

Miles came into the kitchen, a glass of whiskey in one hand, a bottle in the other. The old man followed him, his face a little flushed, his eyes brighter than they had been before. His eyes fixed themselves on Tag and stayed. A little smile appeared on his mouth.

Miles sat down. He slammed the bottle down on the table in front of him with a crash. Cass looked at Miles. Miles caught the look and his scowl deepened suddenly. He sat there glowering for a minute or two. Then he got to his feet.

"I don't want any supper," he growled, and picked his bottle up. A bit unsteadily, he crossed to the kitchen door and went outside. His steadily cursing voice was audible, diminishing as he crossed the yard toward the enormous barn. It was lost, finally, in the clatter of dishes as Wong began to put their supper on.

CHAPTER FOUR

After supper, Cass and Tag accompanied the old man on a walk around the yard. Once Tag started to take the old man's arm, but Cass shook his head and Tag let Emmett Landry walk on alone.

Tag talked steadily, wanting to avoid any questions his father might decide to ask. He did not tell of going south into Indian Territory when he first left home, angry and bitter and childishly hurt. He did not tell about meeting Quinlan and Leach and Sierra and Romolo or about the Kansas bank. Instead, he began his narrative after the holdup of the bank. He began his story with his arrival in eastern Colorado where he took a job riding line for a rancher there.

A couple of times Cass looked strangely at him, as though doubting the truth of his narrative. Both times he stared back steadily, almost defiantly until Cass looked away again.

He was bitterly ashamed of his participation in that bank robbery. He was guilt-ridden over the death of the guard Quinlan had shot. He was even more ashamed of the motives that had driven him to participate originally.

But the robbery was in the past. It was two years in the past. He had not shared the money, nor had he shot the guard. He would have done anything he could to atone for his participation. But he couldn't undo what had been done. He couldn't completely cleanse the slate. All he could do was try to make up for his mistake by the way he lived from now on. All he could do was make sure the mistake didn't compound itself.

His voice droned on as he told his father of places he had worked and of people he had met. His mind was otherwise occupied. He was thinking about Leach, whom he had seen in town. He was remembering Quinlan and Sierra and Romolo. He knew he was going to see them all again — and soon. He knew that as surely as he had ever known anything.

Emmett Landry tired long before the sky was completely dark and the three returned to the house. Taggart got a bottle and three glasses and poured them all a drink. The old man stared at his son soberly over the rim of his glass. His eyes brightened a bit and at last he said, "Welcome home, Taggart. Welcome home."

Taggart nodded, his own eyes burning. The old man drained his glass, put it down, smiled, then turned and climbed the stairs to his room. Tag waited until his door had closed before he turned to Cass. "Is he going to die? Or can he get well?"

Cass shrugged. "I don't know. The doctor said he could get well, only he didn't. It seemed like he just didn't care. Maybe the old boy needs something to fight. Maybe things are too damned tame these days."

“But he’s weak. He’s nothing but skin and bones. That isn’t in his mind.”

Cass said, “I didn’t say it was. He’s weak all right and he’s thin. But part of the reason is that he won’t eat. He won’t eat and he won’t do nothing. It’s like he had decided he was going to die and was just waitin’ for the time to come.”

“Doesn’t he do anything at all?”

“Sits in that rocker on the porch an’ sleeps. Doc says any little old thing could kill him — a shock — a fall — a scare.”

“Then I’d better not let him see Miles and me tangle — if we tangle again.”

“You already have?”

Tag nodded. “As I was riding in.”

Cass frowned worriedly. “Maybe I was rough on you. I don’t know. What I do know is that Miles has been working damn hard since the old man took sick. He’s been working his heart out. Now he thinks you’ve come back to take it all away from him.”

“That isn’t why I came back. Besides, isn’t there room enough on Circle L for both of us?”

Taggart heard the kitchen door slam. He heard the crash of a chair kicked across the room. He heard a bottle smash as it was flung against the stove. Cass shot him a warning glance. Tag watched the door. Miles came through it, his face slack and loose, his eyes burning with fury. He staggered halfway across the room, tripped on a chair and fell headlong.

Cass crossed to him and started to help him up. Miles flung out an arm, catching Cass across the chest and flinging him bodily across the room. The foreman crashed against the wall.

Taggart hadn't moved. Miles looked up, turning his head and peering owlishly. When he saw Tag watching him, his face darkened with rage. He began to curse, in a low, bitterly savage voice, calling Tag every name he had ever heard.

Tag felt the blood draining out of his face. He felt a trembling begin in his knees and arms. He felt wildness coming into his mind and thoughts. Miles wanted a fight; he wanted a fight to the finish. He wanted it and he'd have it eventually, whether Taggart agreed or not. Then why not now? Why not now?

He heard Cass's voice, "Tag! No!"

He glanced at Cass, who was still there against the wall where he had been flung. Cass repeated, "No! He's drunk. He doesn't know . . ."

Tag returned his glance to Miles. He was drunk all right but that didn't mean he didn't know what he was saying. He meant every foul name he had put on Tag; he meant every threat. He wanted a fight with Tag and he wanted his brother dead. There was no mistaking it.

Tag knew if he said anything there would be no stopping it. If he opened his mouth Miles would attack him and he'd have no choice but to defend himself.

Clamping his jaws shut, stifling the anger he felt, he turned and stalked to the door. He flung it open and plunged outside. He rushed blindly away from the house, the sound of Miles's hysterically shouted curses filling his ears, fading only when he had put a considerable distance between himself and the house.

After that he walked the empty plain, wondering how much of Miles's cursing his father had heard. It had been a mistake to come back, he thought, and he ought to go away again. Staying could only mean open conflict with Miles, who seemed bitterly determined to fight with him. Staying could only mean added strain on the old man, for he could not fail to know what was going on.

Yet whenever he thought of leaving, Tag would remember the look in his father's face when he first came home. He would remember the tears shining in the old man's eyes. He would remember the thin and shrunken frame that had been so strong when he left home two years ago.

His absence certainly had not brought on his father's attack. But he had a sudden conviction that if he left again, now, his leaving would be the beginning of the end for the weak old man.

Yet what could he do if he stayed? How could he help Emmett Landry get well? He didn't know the answers to those questions. But he did know he couldn't help his father if he went away again.

With his mind made up, he walked slowly back in the direction of the house. He would stay on Circle L no matter what pressures were put on him to leave. He would stay here, no matter what he had to do, no matter what he had to take from Miles.

The lamps were out in the big house when he returned to it. The whole ranch was dark. He went into the kitchen, struck a match and lighted a lamp.

Carrying it, he went into the living room and up the stairs.

He could hear his father snoring softly in his room. He could hear Miles's heavy snoring where he had collapsed. He wondered briefly if Miles was capable of killing him while he slept. He was horrified by the thought. Miles was his brother. What was the matter with him to make him wonder such a thing?

Yet he knew the thought was not as farfetched as it might seem. Miles *was* capable of killing him in his sleep, or of ambushing him somewhere out on the empty reaches of the ranch. Miles was capable of anything. He was all but out of his mind with rage and jealousy.

Tag closed his door and looked around the room. It was exactly as he had left it two years ago. The same coverlet was on the bed. His shotgun and an old twenty-two rifle still stood in the corner. The shelves standing against the wall were still filled with the books he had read as a boy, with trophies — an old Indian tomahawk, the handle all but rotted away, a collection of arrows and a bow, a single, worn moccasin. Hanging on the wall was a bleached buffalo skull with the horns attached.

He crossed the room and opened the window. The air blowing off the vast acres of grass came into the room, bringing its own free fragrance along with it. He returned to the door and bolted it. The bolt wouldn't keep Miles out if he wanted to come in but it would force him to make enough noise to wake him up. Half ashamed of himself, Tag unbuckled his gun belt and laid it on the nightstand beside the bed. He sat down and pulled off his boots.

In spite of Miles, in spite of everything, there was a warm, good feeling about being home, about being where he belonged. He stood up and removed his clothes, then blew out the lamp and got into bed. But he did not sleep immediately. Instead he stared at the ceiling, feeling the cool night air blowing from the window, remembering his mother. He remembered her vaguely, but only vaguely, for she had died when he was five. He remembered the Indian attack on the ranch in '65, but he recalled that only vaguely too, the fires, the smoke, the shooting and the biting smell of powdersmoke. He recalled his own terror and remembered his father, calm of eye but thin of mouth and angry, though never too angry to reassure his sons.

He remembered the sum of his twenty-four years and the memories were sharp and clear, like the smell of goose cooking on Christmas day or the savage bite of a forty-below-zero wind. He remembered, and remembering all those good things that were now in the past, he fell asleep.

He awoke just before dawn and laid still a moment, staring at the gray square that was the window, listening to the sound of Wong starting a fire in the kitchen stove.

Then he remembered where he was and got up immediately, dressed, buckled on his gun and went downstairs. Wong grinned at him as he passed through the kitchen on his way outside. He crossed to the pump and stuck his head beneath its spout. He lathered with soap, rinsed, then dried his face and hands and combed his hair. Returning to the house, he poured a little warm water into a pan, carried it out on the back porch to where the shaving mirror was.

He got his razor out of his saddlebags lying on the porch. By the time he had finished shaving the sun had turned the few eastern clouds a light, warm pink. He could smell coffee and feel the heat of the roaring stove. He went in and sat down at the table and after a few minutes Wong brought a cup of coffee to him.

He heard heavy footsteps on the stairs, glanced up and saw Miles come into the room. Miles was red-eyed, and squinting like he had a monstrous headache. He scowled at Tag. "You still here?"

Tag did not reply. He watched Miles warily, still wondering at the hate Miles so obviously felt, still wondering what he had done to deserve such a hate. Miles went to the stove and poured himself a cup of coffee. He laced it liberally with whiskey that he poured from a bottle he had brought into the kitchen with him. He sat down at the end of the table and sipped the coffee. Staring at the cup he said savagely, "You be off Circle L by night, you son-of-a-bitch, or I'll kill you on sight."

Tag stared unbelievingly at him. "You'll what?"

"You heard me God damn you! I'll kill you on sight!"

"Why? For God's sake why? Just for coming back? Good Lord, Miles, I've got as much right here as you do. It's my home too."

Miles raised his head and stared malevolently at him. He gulped the rest of the coffee, then picked up the bottle and went outside. On the stoop he stopped, uncorked the bottle and took a long, deliberate drink.

Tag looked at Wong. "How long has he been like this?"

"Just since you come home, Mistuh Tag. Not like this before."

Tag got up and went to the door. He stared outside. He could hear Miles shouting at the men in the bunkhouse. He saw Cass come from the bunkhouse door and cross the yard to him. The two had a violent argument, the words of which Tag couldn't hear.

At the end of it, Cass stalked furiously away and Miles stood there and had another drink. Cass spoke to one of the hands and the man went into the barn, emerging several minutes later with a saddled horse. He brought the horse to Miles, who snatched the reins furiously out of his hands. Miles mounted and raked the horse savagely with his spurs. The animal reared, and then began to buck.

Taggart watched in awe. Miles rode with the reins in one hand, the bottle in the other, and he raked the horse viciously with his spurs at every jump. The horse bucked across the yard and back again, and stopped at last to stand trembling.

The horse had had enough but Miles had not. Again he raked the horse cruelly with his spurs and the horse bolted from the yard and out across the plain. Tag watched until man and horse had become only a speck against the plain.

He returned to the table and sat down, frowning worriedly. Cass came in, glanced at him, then went to the stove for coffee. He filled a cup, crossed to the table and sat down facing Tag. "Did you see that?"

Tag nodded soberly. He stared puzzledly at Cass. "What in God's name is the matter with him? There had to be more to it than just my coming home."

Cass said, "I was hoping you could tell me what was eating him. He wasn't like this when you went away. Why should he change so suddenly?"

Tag did not reply. There was no answer he could make.

Cass said, "And drinkin' too. Lord, he must've started drinkin' as soon as he got up."

"He had some in his coffee. Then he had another one just outside the door. Does he always drink like this?"

Cass shook his head. He studied Tag thoughtfully, as though wondering if Tag knew something he wasn't admitting he knew. At last, apparently satisfied that Tag did not, he said, "You watch him, Tag. You watch yourself every minute of the time. The way Miles feels, there's no telling what he's going to do. He might take it out on himself and stay drunk all the time. Or he might take a notion to get rid of you any way he can."

Tag said, though not believing it, "He wouldn't do anything like that."

Cass shook his head worriedly. "Don't count on it. I sure as hell wouldn't count on it."

Wong served breakfast and both Tag and Cass ate quickly and silently. When they had finished, they both went outside. Cass crossed the yard to the bunkhouse to issue his morning orders to the men.

Tag stood on the back porch in the sun and stretched. He breathed deeply of the high, Wyoming air. It was good to be home. But a good part of its pleasure had been killed by the behavior of his brother. He couldn't understand it. He couldn't understand it at all.

CHAPTER FIVE

Taggart spent that first morning with his father. The old man got up at seven and came downstairs. There was better color in his face than there had been yesterday. His eyes seemed bright. Tag said, "How long since you've been on a horse?"

Emmett Landry frowned. "I can't remember. Seems like years."

"How about a ride today? I want to look around and I don't want to ride alone."

The old man looked at him doubtfully. At last he nodded. Tag went out and saddled horses for them both. When he returned to the house, his father had finished breakfast and was ready to go. He mounted stiffly. Tag followed suit, and they rode slowly out of the yard, out onto the seemingly endless miles of grass. Emmett Landry asked, "Where's Miles?"

Tag hesitated, and finally said cryptically, "He rode out earlier."

The old man accepted the explanation without question. Tag watched him whenever he could without being observed. He wasn't sure he was doing right in getting his father on a horse. But he did know the old man had been dying by inches in the rocking chair on the porch. He did know that if he stayed in that rocking chair it was only a matter of time.

And he remembered a different sort of man. He remembered a man who looked at everything around him as though he owned the world. He remembered his father's eyes being sharp and competent, calm with inner certainty. He remembered a rangy, bony body that once seemed to be capable of anything. He wasn't fool enough to believe his father could ever be the same as that again. But neither did he believe the old man had to spend the rest of his life in a rocking chair.

For a couple of hours they rode, sometimes talking about some little thing they both remembered from the past, sometimes talking not at all. Emmett Landry seemed happy and relaxed, but Tag was not. The memory of Miles riding drunkenly out this morning lingered like an uneasy presence in his mind. And the memory of Miles last night . . . What the hell was eating his brother? What was bothering his brother and what could he do to set things right?

He had no answers for his questions and he didn't dare mention the problem to his father. Furthermore, there was the memory of Leach sitting in the saloon in town, looking at him in such a peculiar way. Coming home was not going to be as simple as it had seemed at first. Staying at home was likely to be extremely difficult.

He brought his father back into the yard an hour short of noon and watched the old man dismount wearily and go inside for a nap. He led the horse his father had ridden to the corral and turned him in.

Then, on impulse, he swung his own horse around and headed straight for town. If Leach meant to make trouble for him, he wanted to know it now. He wanted to know so that he could be on guard.

It was mid-afternoon before he arrived in town. He went straight to the Buckhorn, dismounted and tied his horse.

Sam Leonard was sweeping the floor when he entered. He left his broom and went behind the bar, drew a beer for Tag, and another for himself when Tag invited him to. He came down the bar carrying both mugs, took a long drink then wiped his streaming forehead with the back of his hand. "Hot, ain't it?"

Tag nodded.

"How's things out home? How's the old man?"

"All right. I got him on a horse this morning and we went for a ride."

"Good. I'm glad to hear it. Maybe all he needed was to have you home."

Tag nodded. He said, "There was a man in here yesterday while I was here . . . he looked familiar to me someway or other but I'm damned if I can place him. Did he tell you his name?"

Sam Leonard glanced at him resentfully. "He didn't tell me his name, but I remember who you mean. Man with a brown mustache. He bought me a drink right after you went out of here. We talked a bit. Then Blossom came in and caught me drinkin' . . ." He glanced around uneasily, gulped his beer and put the mug out of sight beneath the bar.

Tag asked, "What'd you talk about?"

Leonard frowned faintly. "You mostly. He asked about you and I told him your name."

Tag's voice was sharp. "What else?" He realized how sharp his voice had been and said more softly, "Was that all he wanted to know about me?"

"Just about. He tied your name in with the name of the town and I told him about Circle L."

Tag had a sinking feeling in his stomach. This was exactly what he had feared. Leach had questioned Leonard and had found out that Tag was the son of Emmett Landry, who owned Circle L. He had also, no doubt, found out how wealthy a ranch Circle L was. He asked, "Where'd he go then, Sam?"

Sam shrugged. Tag finished his beer, paid, and went outside. He stood for a moment on the walk in the blazing sun. Leach might be at the hotel, but he probably was not. He probably had already left town. Tag's eyes stopped on the telegraph station and he immediately walked that way.

The place was cool, almost dark after being in the blazing sun outside. The instrument clacked away, beating out some message or other. After several moments it stopped and the operator turned his head, peering from beneath a green eyeshade. "Tag! When did you get back?"

Tag advanced to the counter and stuck his hand across. Frank Hannen was a little, graying man, a bachelor who liked kids. He was always buying hard candy for them and he'd bought candy for Tag years ago when Tag was small. Tag said, "Yesterday. How've you been, Frank?"

"Fine, fine. I never change." He shook Tag's hand enthusiastically. "What can I do for you?"

"Was a man with a big brown mustache in here yesterday?"

Hannen nodded. "Uh huh. Leach was his name. Know him, do you?"

"Might. Send a wire, did he?"

"Yeah. Funny one too."

"What did it say?"

"I ain't s'posed to . . ." Frank stopped and grinned. "Hell, I guess that don't apply to friends of mine." He ruffled through a pile of yellow papers and brought one out. "Here it is. See what you can make of it." He handed it to Tag.

Tag read it swiftly. It said, "Our Kansas friend is here. Suggest you meet me in Cheyenne. Might be profitable for all of us." It was addressed to Arch Quinlan, Chadron, Nebraska.

Frowning, he handed the paper back. "Guess I don't know him after all. The name Leach doesn't ring any bells. Neither does that telegram. Anyhow, I guess he's gone to Cheyenne." He forced himself to grin at Frank. "Thanks, Frank. Take care of yourself."

"Yeah, Tag. You do the same. Say hello to your Pa for me."

"I'll do that." Tag went out. He felt cold, and the sun didn't seem able to warm him up. Leach and Quinlan would be back in a day or two. They'd probably bring the others along with them. They'd blackmail him, threatening to expose his part in the Kansas robbery if he did not pay up. What they would want was anybody's guess. Some cattle, maybe. Some money that they'd expect him to steal from the old man's safe.

He thought, "If I leave right now, they won't be able to blackmail me. There won't be a damned thing they can do." But he knew that wasn't true. Quinlan and Leach wouldn't give up that easily. They'd go to Miles or the old man, threatening to inform the law of his participation in the Kansas bank robbery if they did not pay whatever amount was asked.

He scowled bitterly. His going away and the news of his crime coming from Quinlan and Leach would be enough to finish the old man off. He stared at his horse unseeingly for a long, long time. Then, wearily and almost listlessly, he untied the animal and mounted him. He turned the horse's head toward home. He would have to stay. He would have to face Quinlan and Leach when they came and outwit them if he could, or pay them off if he must. There was no other way.

From Landry to Cheyenne it was a distance of a hundred and seventy miles. At a leisurely pace, on horseback, it was a three day trip. A man could make it in two, however, if he really wanted to, by starting early in the morning and traveling until late at night. Two days going, two days coming back, and maybe a day in between, Taggart guessed when he saw the two horsemen approaching the ranch five days after he'd questioned Sam Leonard and Frank Hannen about Leach.

The distance was so great, at first, that he could not recognize either of them. But as they drew closer, recognition became possible. Especially for someone who had known them as well as Tag had, who had ridden with them, who had learned to fear and hate them for their ruthlessness.

He swung to the back of his horse and rode out to meet them, wanting neither his father nor Miles to see them here. That familiar, mocking, half-smile was on Leach's face. But Quinlan's face was hard, his eyes bright and glittering. He nodded at Tag curtly.

He was not an exceptionally tall man, nor an exceptionally heavy one. Compact would be a good word for him. Compact the way a panther is compact, composed of muscles that were like fluid steel and always seemed gathered and ready, the way a horse's muscles are gathered just before he begins to buck.

Quinlan's face was broad, almost flat, with square jawlines that ended in a jutting, clean-shaven jaw. His nose had once been broken in a fight, and now spread slightly, giving him a threatening, ugly look. His mouth was thin and wide, but it was his eyes that caught and held Taggart's glance — the coldness in them, like the eyes of a cat, without any feeling, without any warmth. Quinlan said, "Well, well. Damned if it ain't young Tag. We missed you when we split up the loot from that Kansas bank job, Tag."

"I'll bet you did."

Quinlan raised his eyebrows quizzically, but his eyes remained cold. "That's no way to talk, young Tag. You got two, three hundred dollars coming to you."

"And you came to bring it to me, I suppose."

Quinlan's wide mouth made a humorless grin. "Not exactly, Tag. Not exactly. We came to give you a chance to share your good fortune with us. I understand you're about to inherit all this land. And thousands of cattle, too. To say nothing of a good bit of hard cash in the bank."

"Blackmail."

"In a word. Maybe as good a word as any for what we've got in mind."

"Where are the other two, Sierra and Romolo?"

Quinlan grinned at him. "They're back in town." His grin widened. "You never did like those two, did you Tag? Can't say I blame you much. But they're good men in their way. Sierra can pin a mouse to the floor with that knife of his from clear across the room. Romolo can knock a bird's head off with a bullet at a hundred feet. They're good men to have around."

Tag stared at him steadily, uneasiness increasing in his mind. He could see Quinlan following his thoughts. Quinlan said thinly, "Sure you could, Tag. You could agree with whatever we propose, let us ride away and then get your crew together and run us down. You could see to it that we get killed. But there are still the other two, Tag. Romolo and Sierra. They'd get you if you did a thing like that. They'd get you if it took a hundred years. And they'd get everyone connected with you. Your father, your brother. Everyone."

"What do you want?"

Quinlan looked at Leach. "We haven't really decided yet, have we Leach? So far we've been like kids standing in front of a candy store looking at all the good things inside. As soon as we decide what we want, we'll let you know. All right, Tag?"

Tag said thinly, "I just came back. I'm the youngest son. I don't have control over anything. I don't have any money and I couldn't give anyone a bill of sale on anything because I don't own anything."

"You make it sound kind of discouraging, Tag. But we don't discourage easily. We'll think of something. You wait and see."

Tag stared steadily at him. He had been deathly afraid of Quinlan two years ago. He supposed he was still afraid of the man. But it wasn't the same as it had been before. It wasn't the paralyzing fear of a boy for a dangerous and merciless man. Now it was the kind of fear that breeds caution and respect but does not paralyze. He could fight Quinlan, today or any other day, with guns or fists or knives. He might not be able to defeat him but he could sure give it a damned good try.

The trouble was, a good try wasn't going to be enough. For his father's sake, for Miles's sake and for his own, he had to win. He had to defeat Quinlan and Leach and the other two or be destroyed himself, along with his father, and Miles, and Circle L.

Quinlan's eyes stayed cold. Leach's still held that smiling, mocking look. Quinlan said softly, "We'll go back to town now, Tag. But I don't think I want to turn my back on you. Not the way you're looking at me now. Suppose you just ride away from us. You turn your horse and ride back there to the house."

Tag scowled at him but he turned his horse and rode away. And he did not look back. When he reached the house and did finally turn to look, the pair were only two specks in the distance, two specks with a thin, dust trail rising from the plain behind.

But those two harmless looking specks could destroy him and everyone close to him as well. There was no doubt of that. He supposed he'd hear from them sometime in the next few days when they had decided what it was they wanted from him. When he heard from them he'd either have to have some way of beating them worked out or else he'd have to do exactly what they told him to.

His father was standing on the porch. He glanced at the rocking chair and then at Tag. He glanced past Tag at the two specks, now disappearing toward town. "Friends of yours?"

Tag shook his head. "I know them is all."

"Have a fight with them?" The old man's eyes were sharp, sharper than Tag had seen them since coming home.

"Not a fight. An argument." He didn't elaborate. He could see his father's curiosity but he knew his father wouldn't pry.

The old man said, "Need some help with them?"

Tag grinned in spite of the worry eating away at him. It was good to see the old man standing there. It was good to hear him offer his son his help. A helpless man cannot offer help.

Tag said, "I can handle it."

But he wondered if he could.

CHAPTER SIX

During the ensuing week, little was changed on Circle L. Miles seemed determined to drug himself, every waking moment, with alcohol. He was ugly and bad-tempered when he was drunk, but he turned his rage inward now and there were no more quarrels or incidents. Miles seemed unable to decide what he should do. Eventually he would decide, thought Tag, and then the showdown between his brother and himself would take place. In the meantime a restless and uneasy peace prevailed.

Taggart realized he was getting moody too. If his brother's waking moments were occupied by drinking, his own were occupied by worry — about what Quinlan and the other three were going to want — and about what he was going to do about it when they did make known their demands. At last he could stand it no longer — the waiting, the wondering. He saddled up a horse and rode to town. It was mid-morning when he arrived. He sat his horse at the edge of town, looking down at it just as he had when he first arrived two weeks ago. The town drowsed peacefully in the morning sun. A horse stood before the jail, reins looped over the rail, head hanging, tail switching indolently. It seemed incredible that the unholy four were here, so threatening, so menacing.

Sitting there, frowning at his thoughts, he realized something he had not realized before. By coming here to ask what the four wanted of him he was agreeing to their demands, provided they were not too unreasonable. He was agreeing to let the four men blackmail him. And even Tag, with his limited experience, knew that was a mistake. You do not appease a blackmailer. You do not pay him off, for by doing so you pave the way for further demands to be made on you.

Yet Tag was in a position occupied by many before him, a position that would be occupied by many after him. He had no choice. The alternative to paying blackmail was unthinkable. It was his father's death. He was firmly convinced of that. If Quinlan and the others exposed his part in the Kansas bank robbery, he would be sent to prison for a long, long time, even if he escaped being hanged. In his present condition, Emmett Landry couldn't stand such a shock.

He urged his horse into motion again and moved on down the street. He passed the sheriff's office with only a brief glance, then went on to the hotel. He swung down, tied his horse and went inside.

The clerk was a young man Taggart didn't know. Yes, he said, Quinlan and Leach and the other two were registered. But they had gone out. They were probably in one of the saloons. That was where they spent their time.

Tag went out into the street. Standing there, he had a sudden compulsion to mount his horse and return to the ranch. But he resisted it. Waiting, delaying, wasn't going to change anything. The clerk would tell the four he had been asking after them.

He turned and headed down past the jail toward the Buckhorn. As he passed the open door of the sheriff's office, he heard the sheriff call, "Mornin', Tag. How's your Pa?"

He stopped reluctantly and went inside. He nodded at Lew Wintergill, sitting in the swivel chair with his feet up on the desk. He said, "He's better, Mr. Wintergill. At least I think he is. He's been riding a little every morning, and walking some. I think his color is better than it was when I came home. And he's eating better all the time."

Wintergill peered closely at him. "Glad to hear it, Tag. Maybe all he needed was to have his son come home."

Tag stood there uneasily for a moment or two. Wintergill certainly knew that Quinlan and Leach and the other two were here in town. He was smart enough to know what kind of men they were. The minute Tag found them and talked to them it was going to stir the lawman's curiosity.

He stood there awkwardly for several moments, not knowing what to say, disturbed by the penetrating quality of the sheriff's glance. At last he said, "I'll tell Pa you asked after him," and escaped hurriedly. He went along the street toward the Buckhorn, knowing that was the place the four were most likely to be. It was where he had first seen Leach. It was where Leach and the others would probably be waiting for him.

He pushed open the doors and stepped inside. He saw them immediately, sitting at a corner table at the far end of the room. They were playing poker and there was a bottle in the center of the table.

Tag went to the bar. His stomach was jumping. He knew he was doing the wrong thing just by being here yet he also knew there was nothing else he could do.

Sam Leonard glanced at him. "Hello Tag. What'll it be?" His glance sharpened as he saw the expression of Tag's face but when Tag said, "Beer," he drew one and leveled the head with his stock. He slid the mug expertly along the bar without spilling a drop. Tag laid a nickle down and picked up the mug. He took a long, cold drink, then turned and crossed to where Quinlan and the others were.

Quinlan stared coldly at him. Leach, as always, wore a mocking expression. Romolo's face was expressionless as he said, "Hello, Tag. Long time no see. How come you didn't show up in the territory for the split?"

Tag didn't bother to answer the question. Sierra was smiling at him, his teeth white in his dark face. His hair was long as an Indian's, but straggly and unbraided. Sierra smiled and smiled until Tag wanted to smash his smiling face with a fist.

Quinlan said, "Come to see what we want? Is that it?"

"Maybe. What *do* you want?"

"We ain't going to be greedy, Tag. I been thinking on it. I've always wanted to start me a spread down in the Nations an' go straight. Man gets tired of runnin' all the time."

Tag watched him uneasily, suspiciously. Quinlan grinned at him but it was a cold grin with no humor in it or behind it. Tag asked, "So what is it you want?"

"Just a start, Tag. That's all. There's four of us. I figure it would take at least three hundred cattle to make any kind of living for the four of us. Even just to start out with."

"So you want three hundred cattle from me?"

"Tag, you catch on quick."

"I can't give you cattle off Circle L. I don't own them."

"Oh we'll take 'em, Tag. You don't have to give 'em to us. All you've got to do is see to it nobody's around when we do."

"And if I don't?"

Quinlan's eyes were like bits of slate. Sierra got lazily to his feet and edged around in back of Tag. Romolo pushed his chair away from the table far enough to give his gun hand room. Quinlan said, "Your old man's too sick to stand a shock like findin' out his favorite son is an outlaw — wanted in Kansas for bank robbery and murder." His voice was low — only loud enough to carry to Tag's ears, but not loud enough to be understood by the bartender.

Quinlan let his cold glance rest on Tag for a long, long time. At last he said softly. "But if tellin' him ain't enough to finish him off, there's sure as hell other ways. There's Sierra or there's Romolo."

In Tag, suddenly, there was only fury, pure, undiluted rage. In his mind was a picture of his father, and of

Sierra, smiling, smiling, the gleaming knife in his hand . . .

Suddenly he seized the table edge, lifting violently as he did. The table upset, dumping both Quinlan and Leach to the floor. Romolo was far enough back so that he didn't fall.

Tag knew instantly that he was being a fool. He couldn't fight four men, particularly four as deadly as these four were. But he'd started it and now he had to fight. He had no other choice. No other choice. He was getting tired of hearing those three words, even from himself. There had to be some way out. Perhaps not a way out of this fight he'd gotten himself into, but out of the other thing. Warily, he tried to back away, knowing if he touched his gun Romolo would kill him on the spot. Romolo's chair was tilted slightly, but his gun hand hung like a claw over the handle of his holstered gun. Tag had seen Romolo draw and shoot a time or two. The man could get off a bullet faster than a rattlesnake could strike.

He turned his head and glanced behind. Sierra's knife was out, gleaming in his hand. He was still smiling but there was a difference about his smile. It was a little bit more tense. It was an anxious smile.

Tag felt like shuddering. Quinlan got up, cursing steadily. For once the mocking expression had disappeared from Leach's face. Something pricked Tag in the small of his back. He winced because he knew the knife prick had drawn blood. Sierra said softly, "Steady, senor Tag. I will take your gun."

He felt his gun slipped from his holster. The knife was withdrawn but there was a warm spot where it had been, a warm spot of blood. He turned his head and looked at Sam. As he did, Quinlan said warningly, "Stay out of it, barkeep, unless you want your goddamned head blown off." Sam nodded, his face almost gray.

Quinlan came toward Tag. "I figured maybe this would have to be done, young Tag, before you'd do what we told you to. But it's going to be a pleasure just the same." He turned his head and looked at Romolo. "I'll handle him from here on in."

Romolo nodded but his watchfulness did not abate. Quinlan began to advance toward Tag, slowly and deliberately. Sierra stayed behind him and Leach watched from one side, ready to intervene if necessary.

Tag wasn't afraid of Quinlan exactly, but he knew what the outcome of this was going to be. He knew he couldn't win. He had seen Quinlan fight down in the Nations once and remembered that bloody business. Quinlan was like an executioner with those two huge, bony fists. He was as efficient with them as Romolo was with his gun, as Sierra was with his knife. And he enjoyed using them. He enjoyed the bloody smack each time one of them struck. He enjoyed feeling bone break and giving before their force.

Even if Tag could stand against Quinlan and win, there were still the other three. Without Quinlan to hold them back, Sierra or Romolo would kill him. That was another certainty.

Still, he was damned if he'd make it easy for any of them. There was a thing called pride and he was going to take a beating whether he fought back or not. He was going down on the floor of the Buckhorn, lacerated and bloody, battered and unconscious, no matter what he did.

But if he could mark Quinlan . . . If he could mark Quinlan the way Quinlan had marked many another man . . . There would be satisfaction in that. It would make the bitter pill of acquiescence easier to take.

Quinlan had advanced now until he was but half a dozen feet away. Suddenly Taggart rushed, gambling everything on a wild, roundhouse swing that started somewhere behind him and was literally whistling by the time it connected with the side of Quinlan's face.

Striking, it made a sodden crack, and for an instant Tag was certain he had broken every bone in his hand. Quinlan's head, for all the bull-neck supporting it, was snapped sharply to one side, and the man staggered and fell against the wall. He hung there a moment, half conscious but slipping toward unconsciousness.

Tag's hand and arm were a mass of shooting needles of pain. He moved toward Quinlan, knowing this momentary advantage was priceless and not to be thrown away.

Exulting, he stepped in close, readying a second swing, one that would put Quinlan down for good. Too late, he heard someone coming up behind him. Too late, he tried to turn. Out of the corner of one eye he caught movement behind him there, the movement of Leach stepping close, the movement downward of the chair Leach had raised above his head. It crashed down on top of Taggart's head, smashing itself, driving him literally to his knees. He knelt there, knuckles on the floor in front of him, the shattered wreckage of the chair all around him, Leach standing over him. He heard Leach's voice, "The son-of-a-bitch was tougher than Arch figured he was, looks like. Or lucky. But his luck's run out now."

Tag pushed himself to his feet. He stood there, weaving drunkenly. He noticed that Sam Leonard was no longer behind the bar. Or else he had ducked down out of sight. He heard a sound from Quinlan, behind him now, and turned. He saw Quinlan moving toward him, swaying a little, but conscious enough and dangerous. He tried to steady himself, tried to get a swing ready to deliver when Quinlan would be close enough.

He was too groggy and too slow. His fist was hardly clenched and cocked before the monstrous, bony fist of Quinlan smashed into his cheekbone just below his eye.

Now it was Tag who was flung so wildly back. It almost seemed as though his feet left the floor, so powerful was that blow. It brought flashing lights to the field of vision before his eyes. It made Quinlan and the others blur. It made the room go gray, as though darkness was coming down . . .

He smashed against the bar, and hung there, desperately hooking his elbows over it, trying to stay erect. Quinlan advanced on him vengefully, furiously. Never had anyone so nearly put Quinlan out. Tag knew that from the wild and uncontrolled fury in Quinlan's eyes. He knew something else as well — the beating he was going to take here in the Buckhorn would now be the worse for what he had so nearly done to Quinlan.

But he didn't care. He didn't care. He had proved one thing to himself if nothing else. Quinlan could be beaten. So could the other four. They were only men and if he was smart enough, and strong enough, and determined enough, he could beat them as he had so nearly beaten Quinlan here today.

He was thinking that as Quinlan's fist smashed squarely into his face. His head snapped back as though his neck were broken, striking the top of the bar with a loud crack as it did. He slid a little lower, hanging on precariously now, slipping a little more each instant that it took Arch Quinlan to swing again.

This blow took him squarely in the mouth and he felt his teeth give before it, felt blood begin to run from his lacerated lips. But he was sliding down to the floor now. His elbows could no longer hold him up.

He struck the floor, draped over the brass rail at the foot of the bar. Quinlan was cursing, steadily, savagely. He stood over Tag, and he kicked, and kicked, and kicked, until Leach said worriedly, "Hey, don't kill him, Arch. He ain't no good to us if he's dead."

Still the kicks rained against his body, only partially felt because of the unconsciousness creeping over him. But he heard the sheriff's angry roar. He heard a gun discharge and he smelled the acrid powdersmoke. And at last the savage, senseless kicking stopped.

It seemed to Tag that he lay there on the filthy saloon floor for an eternity. Then hands lifted him and he felt himself laid face up on the bar. Someone was washing him, putting something fiery on his cuts, probing his body for broken bones.

He heard voices talking, angrily discussing what had happened here and after what seemed a long, long time, he was able at last to open his eyes. One of them was swelled nearly shut. The other focused on Lew Wintergill's face, immediately over him.

Wintergill whistled softly. "Whew! That was something, Tag, but what the hell was it all about? You know those four bastards, do you?"

Tag nodded. His head throbbed with the movement and he winced. There was no use denying it. It must have been obvious to Sam Leonard that he knew the four.

"What was the fight about?"

Tag shook his head, and closed his eyes, as though it hurt too much to answer questions now. Wintergill asked, "Want 'em thrown in jail? Want to press charges against them for this?"

Weakly, Tag shook his head. He mumbled, "My fight, sheriff. I'll handle it."

Wintergill was silent a moment, but at last he said, "All right, Tag, I guess you know what you want to do. Do you want me to get a wagon and someone to drive you home?"

Tag shook his head, struggling to a sitting position on the bar. He said, "Nope. I can make it home all right." He slid down off the bar, swaying while the sheriff steadied him. When he thought he could make it to the door, he pushed himself away from the bar and staggered out of the saloon.

He turned upstreet toward the hotel, where his horse was tied. It seemed an eternity since he had tied him there. It was a shock to realize it had been less than half an hour.

He untied the horse and hoisted himself painfully to the animal's back. He turned toward home. He'd have to give the four the three hundred cattle they had demanded from him. He had no other choice. There were those three, damned, irritating words again. No other choice. But before he was through he'd change those words. If it was the last thing he ever did, he'd have a choice again.

He felt them watching him as he rode out of town, though he didn't see them and didn't look. He scowled, trying to think, trying to force his brain to work again, to shut out the pain and make his thoughts begin to flow.

Attacking Quinlan had been stupid and had only made things worse. If he was going to outwit the four and defeat them, he'd have to do a better job of it than he had today.

CHAPTER SEVEN

The ride between town and home seemed endless to Tag. His whole body ached and pained. His smashed and lacerated face was worse because these injuries couldn't be hidden either from Miles or from the old man. He'd just have to claim the fight was a personal matter he didn't want to discuss. That might satisfy Emmett Landry but he knew it would not satisfy Miles. Miles would ride to town and ask questions and inevitably he would discover the truth.

Tag had gone no more than a couple of miles before he heard hoofs pounding up behind him on the road. He looked around warily, his hand touching the grips of the gun at his side. To his great relief, the gun was there. The sheriff must have restored it to its holster while he lay almost helpless on the bar.

He recognized Leach as the rider, halted his horse and turned to face the man. Leach reached him and stopped. The mocking look was, for once, absent from his face. He said, "You ought to have known better than that, Tag. Nobody jumps Quinlan and gets away with it."

"I damn near did. I would have if you hadn't butted in and busted me with that chair."

Leach studied him appraisingly. “A lucky punch. That’s what you landed on him, a lucky punch.”

“Maybe.” Tag scowled and the movement of his facial muscles hurt. “What did you follow me for? What do you want?”

“We still want those three hundred head. But now we want a guarantee that you won’t cross us up.” He pulled a paper out of his pocket, unfolded it and handed it to Tag. He followed it with the stub of a pencil that he sharpened with a knife. “Sign that bill of sale.”

“And if I won’t?” Tag hesitated, about to tear the paper up.

Leach stared at him disgustedly. “Why do you have to be so stubborn all the time? Don’t you know when you’re licked? You either sign it or we spill the whole story of that Kansas bank job to your old man.”

“And kill your golden goose?”

Leach nodded soberly. “Like I said before, you shouldn’t have jumped Quinlan the way you did. He don’t much like you anymore. Sign the bill of sale.”

Tag stared at him. He realized neither Quinlan nor Leach would hesitate about exposing him to his father and the law. They’d try to bleed money out of him but if that failed — if he refused . . . He laid the bill of sale against his knee, read it swiftly, then signed it lightly so that he would not puncture the paper with the pencil point. He handed it back to Leach. Leach said, “We came in here from the east, but there’s some rough country to the south. We could see it when the air was clear. You keep your punchers away from that rough country for the next week and we'll get our three hundred head out of there. We'll push 'em down into the Nations and that's the last you'll hear from us."

Tag looked at him sourly. He didn't believe Leach. He didn't believe anyone ever got rid of a blackmailer once the blackmailer had been paid. There was only one way to get rid of these four — devise some way to kill them, to kill all four before any of them could talk.

Much as he hated them, much as he feared them, something within him balked at such cold-blooded murder as that. It balked right now at least. Maybe a month from now — maybe when they came back with a new demand, he would feel differently, able to exterminate them the way he had always been able to exterminate wolves and other predators that preyed on Circle L.

He nodded. "All right. I'm not running Circle L, but I'll try. You tell Quinlan to be careful just the same."

"I'll tell you something instead." Leach's eyes were hard and cold. "Anybody we run into down there gets shot. Is that clear enough for you?"

Tag nodded wearily. "It's clear enough." He watched Leach turn and ride away. He felt helpless, and angry because he did. The bill of sale would protect them legally if they got caught taking the 300 head of Circle L stock. It would also assure them that he wouldn't expose them to the law. Now the trick was to keep everyone out of the rough country south of the ranch buildings for a week. He'd have to think of some way of doing that. His head ached too violently to think. His body was a mass of throbbing pain and so was his battered face. Dully, almost listlessly, he continued on toward home. He approached it from the back side of the house, so that he wouldn't see his father sitting on the porch. He entered the kitchen door almost like a thief.

Wong was working in the kitchen. He turned, his eyes widening, "Hey, Mistuh Tag! What in devil happened to you?"

Tag tried to grin and managed a thin, rueful smile. "Fight, Wong." He went through the kitchen and climbed the stairs wearily to his room. He'd have to show himself eventually but right now he wanted time to think. He wanted to decide how he was going to keep everyone out of that rough country south of here for an entire week. It wasn't going to be easy, particularly since he had nothing to do with the running of the ranch. Miles handled that. Miles and Cass.

Inside his room, with the door closed, he stared into the mirror at his face. He looked at his teeth and wiggled the loose ones with his finger. At least none of them had been knocked out and these loose ones would tighten up in a day or so. He'd had teeth loosened before and they'd always tightened up. The cuts and bruises would heal and go away. But the hatred he felt for Quinlan and the other three would never change.

He crossed to the bed and flopped down on it. He closed his eyes. His head whirled with dizziness, with weakness. There was only one way to manage what Quinlan and the others had demanded of him. He'd have to convince Cass, and his father, that he now wanted to take an active part in the operation of the ranch. He'd have to be on hand each morning when orders were given to the crew. If any of them were sent into the broken country south of here . . . Well, he'd have to figure out some way to stop them, that was all.

He slept, and awoke, and slept again. The second time he awoke it was completely dark. He swung his legs over the side of the bed and sat up. He felt better than he had before, but there was still plenty of stiffness and pain in him.

He went downstairs almost reluctantly, to find his father and Miles in the kitchen eating. He shrugged and sat down. His father stared at him and Miles said nastily, "Well, it looks like you finally got what was coming to you. A long time coming, too, if you ask me."

"Nobody asked you, Miles," Emmett Landry snapped.

Tag looked at his brother who, as usual, had been drinking. He looked at his father. "I'd like to go to work tomorrow. I'd like to start helping out. And I'd just as soon not talk about the fight."

Emmett Landry stared at his son. "All right Tag. Cass assigns the men their jobs every morning. Be on hand tomorrow." He was silent a moment and then he said, "I have been hoping you'd come home and start taking hold. Miles has been handling things but he can't do everything."

"Why the hell not?" growled Miles. "I been doin' all right, haven't I, while you sat easy in that rocking chair?"

Tag said, "Shut up, Miles."

Miles stared at him belligerently. "You going to shut me up?"

Emmett Landry, his face flushed with temper said, "Both of you shut up and quit bickering!"

Tag stared at his father in surprise and so did Miles. The old man stared back angrily. "What the hell are you two staring at?"

Suddenly the pain of the beating seemed like nothing to Tag. The fact that he was being blackmailed seemed like nothing too. The old man hadn't shown this much life since he'd come home.

He put his attention on his food, keeping his eyes downcast so his father wouldn't catch him grinning at the change. More than ever before, he was determined to let nothing upset his father, to let nothing upset him and reverse this apparent trend toward recovery.

Miles was scowling furiously at the two of them, as though this was a conspiracy directed against him personally. Tag forced himself to eat, though every mouthful hurt. He sipped scalding coffee afterward even though it burned his lacerated mouth. His father didn't mention the way he looked again, but occasionally Tag would catch the old man watching him, curiosity and worry in his eyes.

Miles got up at last and went outside, slamming the door furiously after him. The old man said, "He doesn't want you home. He's jealous of you — as jealous as you were of him when you went away."

Tag did not reply. There wasn't much that he could say. His father said, "I've decided something — that a man might as well die in the saddle as sitting in a rocking chair."

Tag looked up and grinned at him. The old man had a long, long way to go, he thought. Deciding to get well was a start but it took a lot more than that.

The old man said reassuringly, "Miles will be all right. He'll get over this after you've been home a while."

Tag nodded. "I hope so. I sure hope he will."

Emmett Landry said, "Guess I'll go on up to bed."

Tag nodded and watched his father get up and leave the room. He heard the old man's steps on the creaky stairs and afterward on the floor overhead. His father was tired tonight, he thought. Healthily tired from the things he had done today, things like walking and riding, and losing his temper at his sons. If he could keep Quinlan and Leach and the other two from spilling what they knew for a few weeks perhaps the old man would be well enough to take the news. Eventually it would have to come out. Tag didn't intend to pay blackmail all the rest of his life.

Right now his problem was to keep everyone out of the country south of here. He didn't want another killing on his conscience. But how? The moment he opposed any of Cass's orders to the men, Miles would take the opposite side as a matter of principle.

He sat idly in the kitchen for a long, long time, watching as Wong cleaned up and did the supper dishes and afterward swept the floor. Afterward he got up and went out, crossed to the bunkhouse and went inside. Cass Borden was sitting at the table puffing on a pipe and reading an old Cheyenne newspaper. Tag sat down across from him. Farther down, at the other end of the table, four or five punchers were playing poker intently. Only two of them even bothered to glance at Tag. Tag said softly, "I want to ask you a favor, Cass."

"Sure. What is it?"

"You'll have to take it on faith and that might be pretty hard to do."

"Try me."

"Keep the men out of that rough country south of here for a week."

Cass frowned and studied him carefully. Tag forced himself to meet Cass's eyes. It wasn't easy. He felt dishonest. Finally Cass asked, "Why? What's going on down there?"

"That's what you'll have to take on faith. I can only tell you this — I've thought it out for a couple of days and I know that what I'm doing is the only thing to do. It's best for —"

"For who? You?"

"For Pa. I'm thinking mostly of him and that's the truth."

Cass studied him for a long, long time, his face doubtful. At last he nodded. "All right, Tag. This place will be yours before too long, yours and Miles's. I guess you got the right to let someone lift a few head of stock if you want them too. Tied in with the beating, isn't it? And with that rough-lookin' pair that rode out here from town?"

Tag nodded. "It's tied in with them. I've got my tail in a crack, but it's the old man I'm thinking of."

Cass nodded. "All right, Tag. All right."

Tag got up, grinning at Cass with gratitude and relief. He started out, and Cass called softly after him. "If you need any help, Tag, you know where to come."

Tag turned his head and nodded gratefully. He went outside. Briefly he wondered why he didn't tell Cass the whole story and let the foreman set up an ambush of the four south of here when they tried to take the three hundred Circle L cattle and drive them off. He shook his head as he walked across the yard toward the house. It wasn't fair either to Cass or to the hands who would have to help to ask them to do his dirty work for him. Besides, even if they outnumbered the four, it would be highly dangerous. Quinlan, Leach, Romolo and Sierra were four of the most dangerous men he had ever encountered. Their dying would not be cheap. They would almost certainly kill several Circle L cowhands before they were killed themselves.

He climbed the stairs to his room, took off his clothes and went to bed. He lay awake for a long, long time, trying to figure some way out of his predicament. He had paved the way for Quinlan and the others to get the three hundred cattle they had demanded of him. But what about their next demand? And the one after that?

He went to sleep at last, after deciding he would take each thing as it came. He couldn't anticipate Quinlan's moves.

Equally difficult was anticipating Miles's moves. He found that out the next morning when Cass issued his orders to the men for the day. Miles waited until Cass had finished, frowning slightly, and then said, "How come you're not sending anyone down into the breaks on Canyon Creek? I told you there were some calves down there that never got a brand on them."

"We'll get to 'em later," Cass said.

"Why later? What's the matter with today? Three men could brand thirty-forty calves in a day down there. And that's about all there are."

Cass turned to the men. "You've got your orders. Get started." His voice was sharp, sharper than it usually was.

Tag looked at Miles worriedly. He hoped his brother would drop it now that the men had started to leave. He watched Miles walk, scowling, toward the corral to get a horse. Cass said, "Something made him suspicious. I guess I didn't handle it very well."

Tag said ruefully, "He's just naturally suspicious with me around." He went back to the house to see if the old man was out of bed. Miles had mounted and now rode out with several of the men.

Tag climbed the stairs and called his father. He crossed to the window and stared outside. He was able to pick Miles out easily and he watched him ride away. Three quarters of a mile from the house, Miles suddenly left the others, made a wide circle and headed south.

Damn! Tag muttered something to his father and hurried from the room. He went downstairs and hurried out. He crossed the yard to the corral, from which he hastily roped out a horse. Cass had already left. So had all the hands. Tag mounted and rode away, heading south.

Miles was already out of sight. Tag scouted back and forth until he picked up his brother's trail. He studied it briefly from his horse's back. Miles had been traveling fast. He'd been holding his horse to a run. Maybe to run the high spirits out of him. Maybe for another reason. Whatever the reason it was going to make him hard to catch. Tag knew he'd have to follow trail. He didn't dare do otherwise. If he lost Miles — if Miles got away from him — he might be killed. Quinlan had meant what he said. If anyone interrupted them while they were rounding up the cattle they intended stealing and driving south, they'd shoot to kill. He knew Quinlan well enough to be sure he'd do precisely what he'd said he would.

He spurred his horse to a lope, which he found was the fastest gait at which he could follow his brother's trail. He kept looking up hopefully, scanning the land ahead, hoping to see his brother and thus be relieved of following trail. But as the morning passed, he knew all chance of seeing Miles was gone. Miles was several miles ahead by now and Tag had no choice but to go on sticking to his brother's trail.

At noon, he struck Canyon Creek. Here, the trail followed the stream east for several miles. Then again it continued south, casting back and forth. It was almost as though Miles had guessed what was going to happen here. It was almost as though he knew.

Tag found his body in early afternoon. He spotted Miles's horse first, grazing in a little, grassy draw.

Scouting in circles, he found Miles lying face downward on the ground.

His chest felt cold and there was a sharpening ache of guilt in it. Miles was dead and it was no one's fault but his. Why . . . why had he let himself be drawn into that bank robbery two years ago? Why had he refused to take his punishment? He should have gone to Lew Wintergill and turned himself in the minute Quinlan and Leach and the other two hit town. His father might have been able to stand the shock. At least his death wouldn't have been certain.

He hurried to Miles, praying he would see movement in Miles's chest. He turned him over carefully.

And suddenly his arms and legs felt like water. He turned weak and wobbly with relief. Miles's chest rose and fell regularly. His shoulder was bloody from a ragged bullet wound, but the bullet had come out. Miles had fainted from shock, and pain, and loss of blood, but he would live. With any luck, Miles would live.

Swiftly, Tag tore his shirt into strips and cleaned and bound up his brother's wound. He led Miles's horse close and with a mighty effort, hoisted and pushed Miles's body up across the saddle. He tied Miles down so that his body wouldn't shift on the ride back to the ranch, which was closer by several miles than town. Then he picked up the horse's reins, mounted his own animal, and headed out toward home.

CHAPTER EIGHT

The ride back home was an agony. He didn't dare go fast, or let the horses travel at a gait that would be hard on Miles. On the other hand, he knew time was important. Miles had lost a lot of blood. He needed better care than the hasty bandaging Tag had given him. He needed rest, and the attentions of Wong, who had treated wounds and injuries on Circle L for as long as Tag could recall.

So he traveled at a walk, with plenty of time to realize that he had brought this trouble home with him. Because of his jealousy of Miles, because of his childish anger two years before, he had let himself be drawn into that bank robbery. Now retribution was coming home to roost. But it wasn't Tag who was paying for his mistake two years ago. Miles was paying, and if he wasn't careful, his father would pay too — with his life.

Traveling in a straight line, and without the necessity of trailing, he was able to return to the ranch in approximately the same number of hours he had used up coming south. Even so it was late when he arrived.

Emmett Landry had apparently not been told that his sons had not come home. He had gone to bed and his room was dark. The only lamp burning was in the kitchen and, as Tag rode in, Cass and Wong came out onto the porch and stared up at him. He slid from the saddle and, with Cass's help, got Miles into the kitchen. They laid him flat on the long table. Wong poured hot water into a pan and was ready with it by the time Tag had removed the bandages.

Cass looked at him from the other side of the table. "What happened?"

"I found him unconscious down near Canyon Creek. I tied him up and brought him home."

Wong was washing the wound. Finished with that, he poured whiskey, straight, over it. Miles groaned and stirred a little, but did not regain consciousness.

Tag felt himself getting dizzy. He picked up the whiskey bottle and took a long drink. He put the bottle down, coughed, and looked at Cass. It was a look that was almost challenging, but Cass didn't take him up on it. Instead he said softly, "Want to tell me what's going on?"

Tag shook his head. "I can't, Cass. It's something I've got to work out by myself."

Cass stared at him. "I've been here on this ranch since you was knee-high to a gopher. If you can't trust me . . ." His face was flushed, his eyes bright with anger.

Tag said miserably, "It isn't that, Cass. It's just that I'm not going to have anybody else getting hurt because of me. It's probably finished anyway. If it is . . ." He glanced up at Cass's angry face. "Don't push me, Cass. Let me try and work things out."

Cass glared at him a moment more. At last he nodded. "But if things get out of hand," he grumbled, "I may butt in whether you want me to or not."

Tag nodded. Before he let Cass and the crew mix in and get themselves hurt or killed, he'd turn himself in to Lew Wintergill for his part in the bank robbery. That might be the best way of handling Quinlan and the others anyway. If he turned himself in he would shift the problem of what to do about them to the law. Then he thought of his father. The shock of seeing his son in jail, of being present at a long trial, of hearing the death sentence pronounced . . . It would be too much for the old man. And then Tag would have his father's death on his conscience as well as the Kansas bank guard's death.

Carefully between them, the three carried Miles to his room, got his clothes off and put him into bed. Wong said, "I stay up a while — maybe sleep in chair tonight." He looked at Tag reassuringly. "He goin' to be all right, Mistuh Tag. You sleep. Don't worry."

Tag nodded. He grinned humorlessly at Wong and at Cass, then went along the hall to his room. He heard Cass's heavy tread on the stairs. He heard the kitchen door softly close.

He got into bed wearily and blew out the lamp. He stared into the darkness for a long, long time. Perhaps it *was* over. He'd given Quinlan and Leach all they had asked him for. Three hundred cattle, even at current prices, amounted to a sizeable sum. Why shouldn't the four outlaws be satisfied? They'd never make that much any easier, or with less risk to themselves.

Yet somehow he knew they would not be satisfied. No blackmailer ever was. Here sat Circle L, a giant to which three hundred cattle was nothing. Here sat Circle L, a ripe plum waiting to be plucked. No, the four would be back. As soon as they had disposed of the cattle, they'd be back. And they wouldn't take the cattle all the way to the Nations, either. They'd sell them the first chance they got. With a bill of sale signed by Taggart Landry, selling the cattle would be a cinch.

He slept, but it was an uneasy sleep, filled with uneasy, jumbled dreams. They were threatening dreams, and although he remembered none of them when he awoke, the uneasiness they had caused in him remained all through the day.

He rode out with the crew, and threw himself into the ranch work almost desperately, as though work could stop his worrying.

This day passed, and the next. Tag's father accepted the story that Miles had been shot by rustlers, that the trail was too cold for following. Miles regained consciousness and, though he glared at Tag every time Tag passed his room, Tag knew he had nothing concrete to tie his brother in with the four rustlers.

A week dragged past. And then, one morning, Quinlan and Leach and Sierra and Romolo rode into the yard as arrogantly as if they owned the place.

The four must have been watching the ranch yard from a distance, so precisely was their arrival planned. Cass had gone. So had all the members of the crew.

But Tag was still at the home place. So was Miles, although he was not yet up. Since he had been wounded, he had not been getting up until later in the day.

Tag saw them from the doorway of the barn, and he stepped outside, standing spread-legged, waiting for them to come to him. Quinlan led the others and reined his horse to a halt a dozen feet away. Leach stayed behind Quinlan. Romolo and Sierra fanned out slightly, one to the right, the other to the left. It was habit that made them do this, Tag knew, the habit of taking all reasonable precautions all the time. Romolo halted his horse so that he could see the house just by turning his head. He kept his right side toward the house, so that he could bring his gun into play instantly.

Tag scowled angrily. "What the hell are you doing here? You got what you wanted. You shot my brother getting it. You could have killed him."

Quinlan said thinly, "I told you to keep everyone out of that rough country for a week."

"I tried but he got suspicious and rode down that way."

Quinlan shrugged. "No matter. We got what we wanted and you found out something — that we mean exactly what we say."

Tag stared at him. "I asked you a question."

"I'll answer it when I'm ready." Quinlan stared harshly at him. Behind Quinlan, Tag could see Leach's mocking face. Quinlan said, "You didn't really think we were going to be satisfied with 300 head, did you?"

Tag shook his head. "I should have known better than to believe a lying sonofabitch like you."

Quinlan's face darkened slightly with anger. He said softly, "The price for keeping us quiet is going up, young Tag. I don't think you can afford to insult us the way you do."

Tag asked sourly, "What do you want this time?" His mind was racing, trying to figure a way out of this. They were nearly fifty yards from the house so it was doubtful if anything said out here could be understood up there. He could expect no help from the house anyway. Only his father, and brother, and Wong were there.

He glanced in the direction Cass and the crew had gone. He could expect no help from anyone. He repeated, "What is it this time?"

Quinlan looked around at the ranch buildings. He said, "It's kind of nice having an interest in a place like this. Makes a man feel good." He swung from his saddle and walked toward Tag.

Tag was furious, and it showed. He said, "Interest hell! You sonofabitch, all I've got to do is go to the sheriff and spill the whole works to him. He'll put me in jail, but he'll get you too. All four of you."

"And your old man will die. If worry about his son gettin' hanged don't kill him . . . hell, there's plenty of other ways." Quinlan stepped closer to Tag, his head thrusting forward threateningly. "You'd better learn to live with us, kid, because we're going to be around for quite a while."

Tag was thinking that he had nearly knocked Quinlan out once — with a lucky punch. He was thinking that if Quinlan wasn't able to order him killed, not one of the other three would dare do it on his own responsibility.

He tensed his muscles and lunged out recklessly. He knew he was a fool but he had reached the place where he didn't care. Getting killed was better than being bled. And once they had killed him they'd have no further hold on Circle L.

His right fist, swung from behind him the way that blow in the saloon had been swung, missed Quinlan's head and whistled past his ear. Tag's momentum threw him against Quinlan and both of them staggered and nearly fell. Tag brought his knee up savagely, and this time was lucky enough to have it connect where it had been aimed. A grunt of pain escaped Quinlan's lips and he doubled, crumpling to the ground.

Instantly Tag rushed him, swinging a foot in a savage kick. He knew he had to keep moving; he had to keep closing with Quinlan. So far none of the others had showed any inclination to interfere and they probably wouldn't as long as Quinlan seemed to be holding his own.

Quinlan caught the foot in spite of his pain and dumped Tag neatly to the straw-littered ground. Tag rolled and came up to hands and knees.

So far he had not been hurt. But neither had he hurt Quinlan seriously. And sanity was beginning to return to his mind. He wasn't helping things by fighting Quinlan here. Even if he didn't get shot for his pains, he couldn't win. They wouldn't let him win. Even if he was able to knock Quinlan out there would still be the other three. But if he could get Quinlan inside the barn

. . . In there, he could find cover for himself from the other three. He might even have a chance to pick them off one by one after he had put Quinlan out of it. *If* he could put Quinlan out of it. The man was getting up, his face still twisted with pain, his eyes murderous. He swung his head and glanced at Romolo and Sierra and Leach. "You stay out of this. I'm going to teach this young bastard something he should have been taught a long, long time ago."

That was something, Taggart thought. At least he needn't worry now about interference from the other three. As long as Quinlan was conscious and able to fight he needn't worry about the other three.

Quinlan came toward him threateningly and Tag retreated, circling as he did until the barn was at his back. He backed in through the door, taking each step carefully. He couldn't afford to trip and fall. Not now.

Quinlan followed him into the barn and the other three put their horses in the doorway from which position they could watch.

Quinlan growled, "Stand still, you goddamned pup!"

Tag stopped his retreat momentarily. He stood there, letting his face show all the hatred and contempt he felt for Quinlan and the other three. He said, "I'm standing. Come on."

Quinlan came in a sudden, furious, reckless rush. It was the kind of rush Tag had wanted him to make because he knew how uncertain was the footing here inside the barn. Straw and manure littered the floor. If Quinlan tried any sudden turns or stops he was certain to slip and fall.

He leaped aside, enough to make Quinlan try to turn. He saw the consternation on Quinlan's face as he realized he wasn't going to make it, as he realized he was going to fall.

And he set himself. He set himself for one mighty blow like the one he'd swung in the saloon in town. Only that kind of blow, squarely struck, would put Quinlan down.

And strike it did. It landed on the side of Quinlan's jaw with a sodden crack. Tag felt the jaw give, felt it crack, and he saw Quinlan flung sideways helplessly.

Tag himself slipped as the blow landed. He went to his knees.

From there, he glanced quickly at the three sitting their horses in the door. It had happened too fast for them to grasp. Quinlan was unconscious but they didn't know it yet.

Tag scrambled to his feet and dived into one of the stalls. He grabbed for his holstered gun.

Dismay flooded him. The gun was gone. It lay, probably buried, out there where he'd been scuffling with Quinlan — out there on the manure and straw-littered floor.

He was trapped here then. Without a weapon, without the means to defend himself. He was trapped in this stall and if he tried to escape it he would be cut down by one of the men in the door.

He'd known he was being a fool when he attacked Quinlan a few minutes before. He hadn't cared, and he didn't really care even now. If they cut him down — if they killed him here, at least their hold over Circle L would be gone. And they'd pay for their crime. Lew Wintergill and a posse would track them down no matter where they went.

They were coming now, coming in through the door of the barn, riding calmly past Quinlan where he lay unconscious on the floor. They were coming without fear and Tag knew they must have seen him lose his gun.

He caught a glimpse of them, then ducked farther down inside the stall. Both Romolo and Leach had guns in their hands. Sierra had his knife poised for a throw.

Tag tensed himself. He wasn't going to crouch here and just let them murder him. He tensed himself to spring up and rush. He might get one of them before he died. He might be able to pull one of them from his horse and kill him with his hands.

But suddenly a shout cut throught the barn's silence from the door. And it was punctuated by a shotgun blast, a blast that racketed deafeningly to the far end of the barn and echoed deafeningly back again. The charge tore a hole in the loft floor above the stall where Tag crouched. Wisps of hay and clouds of dust showered down. The voice had been that of Emmett Landry, sounding as it had twenty years ago; sounding the way Tag remembered it from his years growing up listening to it. It was, for this moment, strong and sure, without weakness of any kind. The old man said sharply in words that cut the silence like a knife, "The next one's going to cut a hole like that in one of you!"

Tag came out of the stall. He saw the barrel of his gun sticking up out of the litter on the floor, went to it and picked it up. He glanced toward the doorway and saw his father standing there, the shotgun balanced lightly in his hands. Emmett Landry didn't take his eyes off the three and he didn't look at Tag. He asked, "Tag, what the hell are these drifters doin' here anyway?"

"They . . ." Tag had been on the verge of telling his father everything but he stopped himself in time. The old man looked strong enough right now to take the news. But how about the trial? And if Tag was executed would he be able to stand that too? Tag didn't think he would. Later, perhaps, if he kept improving as he had been for the last week or two. But not just yet.

He thumbed the hammer back on his gun. Leach, Romolo and Sierra turned their heads to look at him. He raised the gun, leveling it at Romolo's chest and faintly shook his head. Leach looked around at the old man and said, "We used to know your son, Mr. Landry. Quinlan there is carrying a grudge about something that happened down in the Nations a couple of years ago."

The old man said thinly, "Take him and get the hell out of here. Don't come back or I'll blow your damn heads off. Understand?"

Romolo stared murderously at Tag. Sierra and Leach dismounted and helped Quinlan, who was stirring now, to his feet. They supported him between them and helped him on his horse. Still not fully conscious, he clung to the saddle horn as the four rode out of the yard and headed back toward town.

The old man looked at Tag. "Want to tell me what that was all about?"

Tag shook his head.

The old man nodded shortly, broke the shotgun, turned and walked back toward the house. Tag knew he would never mention the episode again.

CHAPTER NINE

Taggart was right about his father not mentioning the episode again. But he could see that it was on his father's mind. Old Emmett Landry was not a fool. He knew there was more to the fight he had interrupted in the barn than a grudge carried here from the Indian Nations and born more than two years before. Ordinary grievances do not endure that long. Besides, there was the matter of the rustling and there was the matter of Miles getting shot.

Worry began to undo the improvements Tag's return had caused in his health. He seemed weaker with every day that passed. He began to sit in the rocker on the porch again. And he watched Tag. He watched Tag with worry and concern in his eyes. Half a dozen times Tag was on the point of telling him the truth, of spilling the whole sordid story to him. Each time he stopped himself. If worry about something he could not understand caused this much deterioration in his father's health, then worry about something real could be ten times worse.

So he kept his silence. But as the days wore on, he became convinced that something had to be done — and soon. If Quinlan and his bunch showed up again, if they caused any more trouble for him and for Circle L, it might bring on the old man's death.

He'd have to get rid of them. Or, failing that, he'd just have to leave again. There was no other alternative. He'd have to lose himself where Quinlan and the others couldn't find him to blackmail him.

To plan their deaths went against his grain. Planning nevertheless, he realized there were only two ways he could manage it. The first of the two offered little chance of success. It was to find each of the four alone, shoot it out and claim self-defense in every case. The trouble with that was that it wouldn't work. All of the outlaws could outdraw and outshoot Tag. It was doubtful if he'd get even one of them before he was killed himself.

The second plan might work if he had the stomach for carrying it out. It was to ambush the four, one at a time. But he knew he couldn't do it. He wasn't made that way.

For a couple of days, he argued out the three alternatives within himself, and he admitted that he couldn't leave. The four outlaws were capable of revenge against Circle L and Emmett Landry if he left the country and thus defeated their plans to get rich blackmailing him. The truth was, he didn't dare to leave.

That left the remaining two alternatives. Shoot it out with them one by one, or ambush and kill them all. The last was still unthinkable. Even if he was able to decide on such a course, he knew when the time came to actually do it that he'd fail. That left only the course he had originally decided upon. Hunt them down and shoot it out. For all its uncertainty, this course offered the best chance of success.

Ruefully, he considered what he meant by success. Not that he would kill all four and escape injury to himself. That was impossible. But the plan itself might succeed. No matter what happened, he might defeat the four. If he killed them and succeeded in claiming self-defense, all well and good. If he did not — if they killed him — then Lew Wintergill would hunt them down. Either way, they'd no longer be a threat to Circle L.

Once he had decided what he must do, he prepared to leave the ranch immediately. He went out to the corral and caught himself a horse. He saddled inside the barn so that he wouldn't be seen, checked his gun and pocketed an extra handful of ammunition. He hung the gun and belt on the saddle horn and left the horse inside the barn. He crossed the yard, returning to the house. He couldn't actually tell his father good-bye. But he wanted to see the old man before he left. He would probably never see him again.

Emmett Landry was sitting on the porch, rocking. Tag frowned to himself as he watched his father from the door. Worry was apparently the thing Emmett Landry couldn't stand. Worry had undone most of the improvement that had taken place in him since Taggart had come home.

He went out onto the porch. "How are you this morning Pa?"

The old man nodded, looking at him with the worry still haunting his eyes. Tag could see how badly he wanted to ask about the four, about the rustled cattle, about Miles being wounded in the breaks of Canyon Creek. Tag said, "You ought to get on a horse and ride for awhile today."

The old man nodded again, but there was no enthusiasm in him.

Tag said, "Stop worrying about that fight out in the barn the other day. It's over. Those four aren't coming back."

Emmett Landry's eyes were sharp and questioning. "Aren't they, Tag?"

Tag said, "No. They aren't coming back." There was conviction in his voice.

His father stared steadily at him. "You in some kind of trouble, Tag?"

Suddenly Tag wanted to tell his father everything. He wanted to tell him about the anger and resentment he'd felt when he'd left two years before. He wanted to tell him how he'd let himself be drawn into the bank robbery because of it. Most of all, he wanted to tell him how terrible he felt about the guard.

Maybe if his father knew the full extent of his trouble — maybe it would give him something to fight and, instead of causing his death, cause him to get well again.

Staring steadily at his father, Tag shook his head almost imperceptibly. He couldn't take the chance. He didn't dare. He'd never know exactly which course was the right one so far as his father was concerned but he couldn't take one that would spare him at the cost of placing a greater burden on the old man's back. He had to do what he honestly thought was best.

He put a hand on his father's thin, bony old shoulder and squeezed it briefly. He smiled. "I'll be back to see you later, Pa. If there's anything you want, yell out for Wong."

"Sure Tag. Sure." The rocker began squeaking again as Tag went back into the house.

For a moment he stood in the doorway, staring at his father's back. Then, decisively, he almost bolted through the kitchen and out of the house by the back door. He strode hurriedly across the yard to the barn. He untied the horse and mounted him. He rode out through the wide barn doors, glanced once quickly toward the house, then headed out toward town, taking a way that would not, at any time, make him visible from the porch. In minutes, he was out of sight.

Miles sat in a chair by an upstairs window of the house, staring moodily at the land outside. There was a brown bottle of whiskey on the table beside him and a cup of coffee that was now half gone.

Miles filled the cup with whiskey, picked it up and gulped it angrily. Miles was always angry nowadays. He was always angry and he was almost always in some stage of drunkenness. He couldn't cope with the problem facing him. It was a problem he couldn't solve. So he drank and hoped that it would go away.

It hadn't gone away. And this morning he was admitting to himself that it would never go away.

Taggart would always be the old man's favorite, Taggart would inherit Circle L when the old man died. And even if a share of it was left to him, the two of them couldn't exist together on Circle L. That was impossible. Hating each other the way they did, it was completely out of the question. Sooner or later one of them was bound to kill the other.

He heard the pound of hoofs and saw Tag ride out of the yard in the direction of town. Tag looked back once, his face seeming white at this distance, as though checking to see if he was observed. Miles's scowl deepened. What the hell was his precious brother up to now? He had looked back almost guiltily, like a kid caught with his hand in a jar of jam.

He got up suddenly. His shoulder gave him a sharp twinge of pain as he did, but he ignored it angrily. He picked the bottle up and took a long drink from it. Then he slammed out of his room and tramped hurriedly down the stairs.

Wong did not look up at him as he went through the kitchen. He slammed the door violently as he went out as though somehow this would even him up with Wong for the cook's failure to speak to him. He crossed the yard. There were still bandages on his shoulder but the flesh was healing well. He felt a little weak sometimes if he tried to do too much, but otherwise he was fine. He got a horse out of a stall in the barn, bridled and saddled him. He mounted and rode out, heading for town along the same course Tag had followed a few minutes earlier. He cast back and forth until he picked up Tag's horse's tracks, and after that followed trail.

There were a lot of questions that needed answering around Circle L these days. Why had Tag tried to keep everyone out of the Canyon Creek breaks the day he had been shot? Who the hell would dare steal from Circle L? Who were those four characters that had ridden out here to see Tag the other day? Four. There had been four of them. By an odd coincidence that was the number of rustlers stealing cattle in the breaks on Canyon Creek, one of whom had shot him from ambush shortly after he picked up their trail. He hadn't seen them — only their tracks — but it seemed damned peculiar that there had been four rustlers — and four strangers out here visiting Tag. It also seemed peculiar that Tag had tried to keep the men out of the Canyon Creek breaks that day he'd been shot, and that Tag had been the one to find him and bring him home.

A lot of questions — questions he wanted answers for. He rode steadily, scowling at the trail he was following, but feeling a touch of hope for the first time since Tag had returned to Circle L. If he could tie his brother in with rustlers . . . Lordy, that would set the old man back on his heels. That would make him take a second look at his precious favorite.

He dug heels into his horse's sides and forced him to a lope. He wanted to have Tag in sight when his brother reached town if possible. He wanted to know exactly where Tag went, to slip in as close as possible and hear what was going on. His shoulder pained him steadily, fiercely, before he had gone half the distance into town. But shortly after he passed the halfway mark, he brought Tag in sight and after that was able to let his horse slow to an easy walk. In mid-morning, Tag rode into town. Miles speeded up a little now, and arrived at the edge of town at a steady lope. He narrowed his eyes as he stared along the street looking for Taggart's horse.

The horse was tied in front of the Buckhorn Saloon. Miles turned the corner half a block before he reached the place, rode half a block, then turned again, into the alley that ran behind the saloon.

There was a shed behind the saloon, and a small yard, which was littered with trash, empty bottles and kegs. He tied his horse to the shed and threaded his way carefully through the trash. He was a little light-headed and his shoulder ached mercilessly, but he didn't think it had bled from the exertion of the long ride here. He thought it had healed sufficiently so that it wouldn't bleed.

He stopped just outside the rear door of the saloon. For a moment he let himself think of Tag, let all his resentment and jealousy renew itself and come boiling to the surface of his thoughts. He lifted his revolver from its holster and looked at it. He spun the cylinder thoughtfully. He realized with a shock that in this instant he could kill Tag. He could and perhaps he would. But not before he had some answers to the questions in his mind.

He opened the door silently and stepped inside. This room was a storeroom, where liquor and supplies were kept. It was piled high with beer and whiskey kegs, with wooden boxes of bottled whiskey. He closed the door as silently as he opened it, and moved forward toward the front part of the room.

Another door blocked his way and he opened it slightly — enough so that he could see through, so that he could hear what was going on. He heard his brother's voice. ". . . Quinlan and his three friends. Have you seen them, Sam?"

"Today you mean?" This was Sam Leonard's voice. "They were in here last night. They're probably still over at the hotel."

And Tag's voice again. "Thanks, Sam."

Miles pushed the door farther open and stepped through into the saloon. Tag was standing at the bar, a beer mug in front of him. Sam Leonard had his back to Tag and was polishing glasses with a towel.

Drawing his gun, Miles walked carefully and silently across the room.

Without hesitation, Miles brought his gun barrel down, raking savagely along the side of Tag's head. Tag's ear began to bleed. He tried to turn, tried to reach his gun but he was partially stunned and slow. Miles brought the gun down for a second time.

This time it was a solid blow, squarely struck. It landed on the top of Tag's head, the sound it made sodden and ugly.

Tag's knees bent. He collapsed, with only the crash of his falling breaking the silence inside the saloon.

Sam Leonard turned. "What the hell . . .?"

Miles said harshly, "This is Landry business, Sam. You keep out of it and you keep Lew Wintergill out of it too."

Leonard came around the bar. He knelt beside Tag. Looking up he said, “You could have killed him with that damned gun.”

“But I didn’t. Keep your mouth shut, Sam, and everything will be all right.” Holstering his gun, he went back out the rear door, got his horse, mounted and rode uptown toward the hotel.

Tag had been asking about Quinlan and the other three. Now it was to the four that Miles meant to go for the answers to the questions in his mind.

Tag wouldn’t have told him anything. He had realized that as he stood there in the back room of the saloon. But Tag’s four friends would talk. One way or another, he’d find out from them the things he had to know.

CHAPTER TEN

Miles Landry went out through the back door, threaded his way around the discarded trash, untied and mounted his horse. Remembering how it had felt hitting Tag with his gun, he felt a solid satisfaction. Tag was going to have the king of all headaches when he came to. *If* he came to. Sam Leonard had said he could have killed Tag with the barrel of his gun.

He shrugged a bit uneasily as he rode down the alley. It wasn't that he cared what happened to Tag but he hoped Tag didn't die from that blow on the head. He didn't want to stand trial for killing him, particularly under circumstances in which he could not claim self-defense.

He rode out into Main Street and headed for the hotel. Tag's horse was still tied in front of the Buckhorn Saloon. Lew Wintergill was sitting on the bench in front of the jail, his hat tilted forward over his eyes. He looked as though he might be asleep.

A waif. A nothing. That was what Miles was. He didn't even know who his parents were or what his real name was. He'd been found by old Emmett Landry years ago in a wagon that had broken down on Circle L's vast range. His parents were gone, and no trace of them had ever been found. Left to die out there, he reflected with bitterness, left to die because no one wanted him. They'd just walked off and left him there in that broken wagon to die.

Landry had told him it was possible they'd tried to get help and had been killed by Indians. Or that they had died from disease. Or that they had simply left to find water, and food perhaps, and had become lost and unable to make their way back.

There were a lot of explanations of what might have happened to them. But the unpleasant fact remained; Miles was a waif, a nothing, a child left to die alone on the plain, too young to even remember his name, too young to remember what his parents' faces had looked like.

Emmett Landry had raised him, Emmett Landry and Emmett Landry's wife. Then Taggart had come along and all of a sudden Miles had felt like exactly what he was, a waif, a cast-off that nobody cared about. Suddenly all the love Emmett Landry and his wife had given him was given instead to the newborn Tag.

Miles resented it. He wasn't very old himself when Tag was born, and he didn't mind showing his resentment. Once he even tried to get rid of Tag by carrying him out and hiding him so that he would freeze to death.

He remembered the incident yet. He remembered the way Tag's mother had set upon him, how she had whipped him, how enraged she had become. He remembered his own awful terror, and the way he'd fled into the open prairie — out into the howling blizzard that had been raging at the time.

Lost, he was, cold, and frostbitten. Lost and full of terror. Then, almost as though he were dreaming, he had heard Emmett Landry calling him. His own voice, calling back, had been snatched away by the wind. Yet somehow Landry had found him, and caught him close against his chest to warm him, and had carried him back to the safety of the house.

After that, Emmett Landry had gone out of his way, had bent over backward to show no favoritism toward his true son, Tag. In fact, thought Miles now ruefully, he'd bent so far over that Tag had felt unwanted and had gone away.

He reached the hotel, dismounted and tied his horse. He stared at the door uncertainly. Something within him told him this was wrong. This was a mortal sin he was about to commit against Emmett Landry and his son. But he shrugged his uncertainty away. To hell with them. To hell with both of them. He went into the lobby and crossed its white tile floor to the desk.

Larry High straightened guiltily from the Wild West Weekly he had been reading. He shoved it under the counter and looked at Miles. "Hello, Mr. Landry. What can I do for you?"

"Those four hardcases — what rooms do they have?"

"Two connecting rooms, Mr. Landry. Seven and nine. You know where they are."

Miles nodded. He tramped across the floor to the foot of the stairs. He ascended, scowling, beginning to feel a little uneasy about his ability to handle the four in rooms seven and nine. The thing to do, he supposed, would be to let on that he knew everything. He could even threaten to go to the law about the rustling. That ought to make them talk. Or make them kill him, he thought, and loosened his gun in its holster at his side.

Determinedly, then, he walked along the hall to a door with a black seven painted on it. He knocked. For a moment there was no sound. Then there were sounds of low voices mumbling, and then footsteps approaching. The door opened. A man stood framed in it, a man that immediately glanced over his shoulder at another standing by the bed. "Let him in."

The one who had opened the door stood aside. Miles went into the room. He stood there uncertainly, looking at the heavy-set man standing beside the bed. This one was apparently the leader of the four. There were two more men in the adjoining room. They came through the connecting door and stood looking questioningly at him.

Miles said, "I know one of you shot me. I don't know which it was, but I know it was one of you. Tag told me that much."

The heavy-set man scowled but none of the four spoke, neither admitting nor denying the accusation.

Miles said angrily, "Damn you, don't stand there like a bunch of wooden Indians. I can turn around and walk downstairs to the sheriff's office if I have to. I can tell the story to him. Do you know what the penalty for rustling is in this territory?"

The heavy-set man said, "I don't know what the hell you're talking about. Get out of here."

The man who had admitted Miles, a slightly-built, dark-complexioned man said, "Maybe we ought to talk to him, Quinlan."

"Shut up, Sierra." But Quinlan glanced around toward the other two. One of them nodded slightly. Quinlan turned back to Miles, still frowning. He asked, "Just what the hell have you got in mind?"

"It could be that we want the same things. Could be we could help each other."

Quinlan turned his back. He walked to the window and stared down into the street. Miles said angrily, "All right. You've got a choice. Either you talk or I go down there and swear out a complaint against the four of you for rustling. And don't say I can't make it stick. I'm a Landry and the word of a Landry carries weight around here. I've got a bullet wound in my shoulder and I'll swear one of you put it there when I caught you rustling in Canyon Creek."

He stopped for breath. Quinlan's back was still turned toward him but there was a changed atmosphere within the room. He couldn't have defined it exactly but it was plain enough. It was a threatening atmosphere and suddenly Miles knew he had never been closer to death in all his life. Not even the time when, as a child, he had been lost on the freezing plain.

He said quickly, "But that ain't what I want. I'm not after the four of you. I want to get rid of Tag."

The man at the window turned. "That's damn funny talk comin' from his own brother."

"I'm not his brother. The old man raised me but I'm no blood kin of Tag's."

Quinlan crossed the room and peered closely at Miles's face. "What you got in mind?"

Miles forced himself to meet Quinlan's eyes. It wasn't easy. Quinlan had a forceful, almost overbearing personality. He inspired fear and Miles was suddenly afraid of him. Miles said, "Depends on what you want, I guess. What *do* you want? More cattle?"

Quinlan snorted but he did not reply. And suddenly Miles knew what they wanted. They wanted Circle L.

He stared at Quinlan unbelievingly. It was impossible. How in God's name did they think they were going to manage that? Quinlan said harshly, "You know what we want. We want part of Circle L."

"You're crazy. You can't . . ."

"Can't we? How do you suppose we got Tag to let us take those cattle down in the Canyon Creek breaks?"

"Blackmail? You know something about Tag?"

Quinlan snorted. "We know plenty about Tag. Enough to . . ." He stopped suddenly, then finished, "Enough."

Miles's thoughts were racing, trying to keep abreast of this. It was incredible, fantastic. It was the most fantastic thing he had ever heard. The silence went on, and on, and at last he breathed, "You'll never get away with it. Never in a million years."

"Won't we?" There seemed to be a lot of assurance in Quinlan and the others, yet suddenly Miles had the feeling they weren't quite as sure of themselves as they seemed. If they had been completely confident, they wouldn't even have bothered talking to him. Nor would they have revealed their plans. They needed him. He said, "Half — I'll give you half. But you'll have to do all the dirty work."

He had their full attention now. And he could see the greedy way they looked at him. Their eyes were shining. One of them, Sierra, licked his lips.

He felt as a man must feel in the instant after he dives off a cliff. There was no retreating, no going back. He was committed, for better or for worse.

He regretted it, suddenly. It was as though he had already killed old Emmett Landry, as though he had already murdered Tag. And now, too late, he realized that they hadn't been so bad to him. The old man hadn't had to raise him the way he had. He hadn't had to raise him like a son. It would have been plenty if he'd just given him food and a place to sleep. Nor had Tag had to treat him like he'd have treated a blood brother.

But it was too late for being sorry now. You do not advance with four like these and then retreat. He said, "The old man's pretty weak. A shock could kill him. Go out there and tell him what you know about Tag. Tell him Tag agreed to your rustling those cattle out of Canyon Creek. Tell him Tag sent me down there after you agreed to kill me for him."

Quinlan nodded coldly. Miles continued, "And if that doesn't do the job, you'll have to find another way." He stared challengingly at Quinlan and at the other three.

Quinlan nodded again. "We'll be taking a chance, doing that."

"You expect to get half of Circle L without taking any chances?"

Quinlan shrugged. "How do we know you'll give us half?"

"I'll sign a deed right now."

Quinlan shook his head. "It wouldn't do any good. You can't deed over something you don't own. But I'll tell you what you can do. You can make out a will, leaving everything to me. Then if you try to go back on your word . . ." He smiled and shrugged. "All I'll have to do is see to it something happens to you."

Miles began to get a cold feeling in his spine. He wished now that he'd never gotten into this. But he had and there was nothing to do but what they asked. He asked feebly, "And what about Tag?"

"We'll take care of Tag."

Miles nodded weakly. "Make out the will. I'll sign it. Then get going and get this over with."

Quinlan nodded coldly. He got a sheet of paper and sat down at the desk. He began to write with the scratchy hotel pen.

CHAPTER ELEVEN

When Quinlan had finished writing out the will, Miles took it from him and read it over carefully. It was crudely worded, but it was adequate. He knew that. He'd once heard of a case where a dying man had scratched out a will in the dirt and it had been adequate.

He sat down at the desk in the chair Quinlan had just vacated. He picked up the pen and dipped it into the ink. In that instant he knew he was a fool. This was not a will; it was a death warrant. As soon as he signed it, he'd be fair game for Quinlan and his deadly friends.

Besides that, even if they didn't kill him, they'd end up owning half of Circle L, and how long could he tolerate four partners such as these?

He hesitated, staring at the pen. The old man was going to die — probably in a matter of months. Circle L would then pass to Tag and to him anyway. Or would it? Maybe the old man had cut him out of his will, or would do so now that Tag had come back home.

He thought of Tag, hating him, letting all the corrosive quality of his hatred work on him. He dipped the pen in the ink again and signed the will.

Quinlan picked it up, crossed the room blowing on the ink to dry it. Miles looked at his face and at the faces of the other three. There was a triumphant quality to their expressions, a speculating quality as they looked at him as though they already were wondering what the best way was for getting rid of him.

Again that coldness began at the base of his spine, traveling upward until it ended with a chill, tingling in his neck. He got up hastily, and literally bolted from the room, slamming the door behind him and running along the hall. He thought he heard someone laugh behind him in the room, but he could not be sure. He ran down the stairs and across the lobby to the door.

He ran outside, not even aware of the two or three people in the lobby or of the way they stared at him. He glanced up the street and down, as though someone already was after him.

Tag's horse was still in front of the Buckhorn Saloon. The sheriff no longer sat on the bench in front of the jail. He had disappeared. He was probably up in the Buckhorn, thought Miles, helping Sam Leonard take care of Tag.

He ducked back into the hotel. There was a saloon connected to the hotel, with one entrance opening onto the street, another to the hotel lobby. Miles hurried across to it and went into the saloon, which was called the Tivoli.

He crossed to the bar and the white-aproned bartender said, "Howdy, Mr. Landry. What'll it be?"

"Whiskey. Just gimme the bottle an' a glass."

"Yes *sir*." Smitty, the bartender, got a bottle and glass and passed them across the bar to him. Miles took them and glanced around the room. He picked a table in a corner nearest the lobby, the most inconspicuous corner in the place. He opened the bottle, poured half a glass and gulped it down almost frantically.

He waited just a moment, until the burn in his throat had passed, until he was able to breathe normally again, and then poured a second glass. He gulped this one similarly.

The third and fourth drinks followed the first two down Miles's throat, and after the fourth the world began to look a little better to him. Maybe things weren't so bad after all. Quinlan and the others would take care of the old man and Tag, leaving him with half the ranch, them with the other half . . .

Suddenly he tensed. His eyes brightened and the look of terror left his face. Wait a minute! Quinlan and the other three men had nothing but the will and, as long as he was alive, the will wasn't worth a damned thing to them. Why couldn't he let them take care of the old man, and of Tag, and then turn them in to the law? Lew Wintergill couldn't handle them by himself but the Circle L crew, and the sheriff, and Miles, could handle them easily.

The ethics of double-crossing Quinlan didn't bother him because he knew they meant to double-cross him first chance they got. The only thing that worried him was getting away with it. He'd need Lew Wintergill, and Cass, and the Circle L crew and he wouldn't get their help if they suspected he was behind the deaths of Tag and the old man. The will . . . it was the only thing that tied him in with the four hardcases and he could claim his signature had been forged. Or he could say he had been forced at gunpoint to sign the will.

He began to feel better almost at once. He poured himself another drink, but he drank this one more slowly than he had the first four. He began to smile; he felt a warm glow come over him. It was not so hopeless after all. There *was* a way out. All he had to do was wait — until they had caused the old man's death — until they had gotten rid of Tag.

Sitting there, sipping his drink, he began to rehearse what he would say and what he would do. And he smiled foolishly as he did, the will that he had at first considered a death warrant forgotten in the excitement of his plans. He was the smart one, he thought to himself. He was going to make fools of all of them, the old man, Tag, and the four outlaws. He was the one that would end up master of Circle L.

He chuckled softly as he poured himself his sixth drink. He sipped it, smiling to himself. Across the room, Smitty and a man standing at the bar were just a blur.

Quinlan waited a moment after the door closed behind Miles Landry. Then he looked at the other three and laughed. "How's it feel to be part owners of an outfit the size of Circle L?" he asked.

Leach was not smiling and there was no mockery in his eyes. He said, "We ain't part owners yet. Just because everyone's acted stupid so far doesn't mean they'll act stupid all the time. Suppose you do manage to kill the old man without layin' hands on him? Suppose you even egg Tag into drawin' against Romolo? That ain't going to keep Tag's brother from double crossin' us."

Quinlan waved the will at him.

Leach snorted. "That's no good to you and you know it ain't. Not for a long, long time. If Miles was to get killed they'd snoop into everything any of us ever did."

Quinlan said, "He won't get killed. For now, we're going to be satisfied with half the ranch. Later, Miles can get stomped on by a horse or something, but by then we'll be dug in at Circle L. They won't be able to blast us out. And we'll have money enough to fight anything they dig up out of the past."

Leach nodded reluctant agreement with this. "Then play it that way," he said. "Don't get greedy and start thinking about getting rid of Miles. Not for a long, long time."

Quinlan nodded but Leach plainly wasn't sure Quinlan agreed with him. Quinlan poured himself a drink and gulped it down. He said, "All right, let's get busy then. Leach, you go down to the livery barn and get our horses saddled up. You and me will go out to Circle L and have a talk with Tag's old man."

Leach nodded. He picked up his hat, hitched at his gunbelt and went out the door. Quinlan could hear his footsteps receding along the hall, then clumping noisily down the stairs. He turned his head and stared at

Romolo. "I want you to be damned careful how you get rid of Tag."

"How do you mean, careful?"

"I want Tag to draw on you and I want you to give him plenty of edge so there won't be any arguments later on. Landry is a big name hereabouts no matter who carries it or what he's done in the past. And I want several witnesses to the fight. See to it there are at least three men present when you fight with Tag."

Romolo nodded and started to turn away.

Quinlan said, "I'm not through yet. Three witnesses, and by that I mean three men who are looking when you draw. So you'll have to get an argument going with Tag before you actually egg him into drawing his gun on you."

Romolo looked slightly puzzled now. "What kind of an argument do I start? Hell, I ain't got nothing to argue with Tag about."

Quinlan smiled thinly. "He's got plenty to argue with you about. Along about now he's going to be thinking of trying to get rid of all four of us. Let him know we've gone out to talk to the old man. Let him know we've got a will that Miles has signed, naming us beneficiaries. If that doesn't egg him into grabbing for his gun, then nothing will. And I don't peg Tag as having any yellow in him."

Romolo nodded. Sierra asked, "What am I supposed to do?"

Quinlan said, "Just be there, that's all. Just be sure nobody interferes. Like I said, Landry is a big name in this town. Those three witnesses might not take kindly to seeing Romolo kill a Landry right in front of them."

Sierra nodded. Romolo went to the door and Sierra followed him. The two went out. Sierra closed the door behind them and Quinlan heard them going down the stairs.

He began to pace swiftly back and forth between the door and the window, frowning to himself. This was the biggest thing he had ever been on. This was bigger than all the bank and stagecoach jobs combined. This, if it came off right, could make him rich all the rest of his life. And it could give him something he had always craved but had never had — respectability, a name and position in the community.

He thought of Leach and Sierra and Romolo. He didn't intend that any of their names should appear on the deed he would get from Miles. He'd take care of them because he needed them. They could stay on Circle L, forever if they wanted to. But not as owners. Only as hired hands. This plan was his — even if Leach had put him onto it.

He paused at the window and stared outside. He saw Sierra and Romolo entering a saloon across the street. He saw Leach come from the livery stable, riding his own horse, leading Quinlan's mount.

He picked up his hat and put it on. He drew his gun from its holster and checked its load, then seated it lightly in the holster again. Smiling at himself for taking the precaution, he went to the door.

He was as nervous as an old woman, he thought. And maybe it was a good thing that he was. Nervous was a good way to be today. Tag had acted stupidly so far and so had Miles. That didn't mean the old man would act stupidly, or that his foreman would.

He went out into the hall, closing the door behind him and locking it. Thoughtfully, he went down the stairs. The clerk spoke to him, his voice holding the usual mixture of fear and respect, but it was a different kind of respect he wanted here. This was respect based on fear — of his gun, his companions, the way he looked and dressed. He nodded curtly at the clerk and went on out.

Leach was sitting on his horse in front of the hotel. Quinlan took the reins of his own mount from Leach's hand and swung to the horse's back. He glanced across the street at the saloon where Romolo and Sierra had disappeared in time to see them reappear. Romolo glanced at him and faintly shook his head. He and Sierra turned and headed for the next saloon, farther down the street.

Quinlan turned his horse away from the hotel and headed out of town toward the buildings of Circle L. Passing the jail, he looked up as the sheriff came out the door.

Lew Wintergill frowned at him. He said, "Wait a minute, you."

Quinlan stopped. The sheriff said, "Something's going on that I don't understand. I don't suppose any of you would know anything about Miles Landry getting shot, would you?"

The question was so abrupt it caught Quinlan momentarily off guard. He knew his expression of surprised innocence was wrong. It was out of character and it wouldn't fool this man. It wouldn't fool him for a minute. He scowled and asked, "Why would we know anything about a thing like that?"

The sheriff shrugged. "I don't know, but maybe I'll find out when I get answers to a couple of telegrams I've sent."

"Telegrams?"

"About you and your friends. Does that worry you?"

Quinlan could have cursed himself for the expression of injured innocence he felt coming over his face. He asked, "Why should it worry me? I've got nothing to hide, sheriff. None of us has anything to hide."

"Then you've nothing to worry about. Nothing but what you do while you're here."

Quinlan was getting angry now. He tried to curb his anger but without very much success. He said sourly, "If you're through lecturing us, sheriff, we'll be on our way."

Wintergill nodded coldly, staring straight into Quinlan's eyes. Quinlan rode on and the sheriff shifted his glance to Leach, as though trying to memorize his face.

Riding on, Quinlan had a bad moment, wondering if he was being smart leaving Romolo and Sierra to handle Tag. Neither Romolo nor Sierra was overloaded with intelligence. Both were deadly and efficient with their weapons, but neither thought things out.

Then he shrugged. He had to trust them to take care of Tag whether he wanted to or not. Getting rid of the old man was going to take more skill than either

Romolo or Sierra possessed. It would take all the skill he and Leach could muster and maybe even then the plan would not succeed. Violence might be necessary, and if it was, extreme care was going to be needed to hide the results of that violence. The old man must appear to have died from natural causes.

He held his horse to a leisurely walk all the way to the end of the street, very conscious of the sheriff's glance on his back. He was scowling all the way and as the pair cleared the limits of the town he growled, "One of the first things I'm going to do when I get my hands on that ranch is get rid of that nosy son-of-a-bitch."

"Who do you suppose he sent those telegrams to?"

"Who the hell could he send 'em to? He doesn't know where we came from when we came here."

Leach frowned worriedly. "I'm not so sure. He got hold of Tag, which meant he must have had some kind of address to send a letter to. Maybe he had Tag's address down in the Nations and maybe that's where he sent his telegrams."

Quinlan scowled at Leach. "Or maybe you've been doing too damn much talking since you've been here. Maybe that was how he knew where to send his telegrams."

Leach shook his head, his face slightly flushed. "I never talk about myself. You know that."

Quinlan said, looking straight at him, "Then we've got nothing to worry about, have we? He can't dig a damned thing up."

Leach did not reply. Irritably, Quinlan spurred his horse. If anything went wrong with this . . . God help anybody who did anything to make this plan go wrong.

CHAPTER TWELVE

The first thing of which Tag Landry was conscious was pain in his head. Excruciating pain — pain like a living thing, like a tangible thing that had size, and shape, and a form all its own. It seemed to fill his head; it seemed to be his head.

He heard a groan, and another, but it was several minutes before he realized the groans were coming from his own lips. Then he was able to see light, light shining through his closed eyelids, but he dreaded to open his eyes because he knew it would increase the pain which was already almost intolerable.

He heard a low voice say, "He's comin' out of it, Sam." And he heard another voice reply, "Thank God! I was afraid . . ."

He opened his eyes, now curious as to whom the voices belonged. He saw two blurry faces, and beyond them light, and he winced as the pain knifed through his head again. He closed his eyes, or almost closed them, leaving only a slit to let in the light. But it was enough to see where he was and to see the two men bending over him.

He was in the Buckhorn Saloon, on one of the tables, which was not long enough for his entire length and so left his lower legs dangling over the edge. The two faces were those of Sam Leonard and Lew Wintergill. Light glinted briefly from the badge on the sheriff's chest as he changed position so that he faced the door.

Tag frowned with his effort to remember what had happened to him. He'd been standing at the bar having a beer when all of a sudden the roof had fallen in on him. Or so it had seemed at least. Something had raked the side of his head, nearly tearing off his ear, and while he was fighting to turn and get out his gun, something had hit him squarely on top of the head and after that everything went black.

He spoke at last, his voice hoarse and low. "Who hit me, for God's sake?"

"Miles." Sam Leonard's voice was outraged. "He just walked up behind you and let you have it with the barrel of his gun."

"Why? For God's sake, why would he do a thing like that?"

Neither Lew Wintergill nor Sam answered him. Tag closed his eyes a moment, then opened them determinedly and struggled to sit up. Lew helped from one side and Sam from the other. Tag's head began to pound with renewed fierceness, and he winced visibly. Spots danced before his eyes and the room reeled dizzily. He said, "Lordy!"

"Don't try getting on your feet just yet. Sit still a minute or two."

He grinned weakly. He had no intention of getting on his feet until he was sure he could stand on them.

Besides that, he was beginning to remember why he was here in town. He was here to settle with the four outlaws, one way or another. He was going to get rid of them, or they were going to get rid of him. There could be no middle ground.

To do so, he would need all his wits about him. He would have to be clear-headed and strong — stronger than he had ever been in his life before — and faster too.

Damn Miles! Damn him anyway! He must have followed him in, must have followed all the way from the ranch. But why? Did Miles suspect what was going on? Was it possible he suspected why Tag had come to town?

He doubted it. He didn't see how Miles could guess a thing like that. Miles might suspect a connection between the four outlaws and Tag. He might also suspect a connection between the rustling on Canyon Creek and the four outlaws. He might be trying to find out which of the four had shot him earlier.

He asked, "Where'd Miles go?"

Sam Leonard shrugged. "Went out the back door, same way he came in. Maybe he went back out to the ranch."

Lew Wintergill peered closely at him. "Want to tell me what's going on, Tag? Might be I could help. Those are four damned hard characters that have been asking questions about you and if you think you can handle 'em by yourself, you're crazy. Besides that, it looks like now you've got Miles on your back too."

Tag made a half-hearted smile. "There's nothing you can do. It's something I've got to handle by myself." He wanted to accept the sheriff's help but he knew Lew Wintergill. Wintergill was so honest that if he so much as suspected that Tag had been involved in a murder and bank robbery . . . he shook his head cautiously.

Wintergill warned, "I may butt in anyhow."

Tag stared at him. For an instant he looked just the way the old man had looked thirty years before. He said harshly, "Don't interfere, sheriff. This is Landry business and none of yours."

The sheriff flushed. His eyes flashed. But he had known the old man thirty years before and he'd never crossed Emmett Landry when he looked the way Tag was looking now. He grumbled, "Who the hell do you Landrys think you are? You may own Circle L, but you don't own the whole county and you don't own me."

Tag did not reply to that. Wintergill grumbled sourly several more moments, then angrily turned and tramped from the saloon. Tag slid down from the table and walked unsteadily to a chair. "Bring me a beer, Sam. Maybe it will clear my head."

Sam Leonard went behind the bar and drew a beer. He brought it to Tag and put it down. He peered at Tag with concern.

Tag's head ached terribly. He knew he couldn't take on Quinlan and his friends feeling the way he did but he also knew he had to do something soon. Time was running out.

He gulped about half of the beer and then deliberately poured the rest on top of his head. It felt cold, and it stung where his scalp was cut, but it helped. It reduced the ache and it helped clear his head. He got to his feet, picked up his hat from the table where Sam had put it and settled it carefully on his head. He hitched at his gun belt and touched his gun to be sure that it was there. He said, "Thanks, Sam. I think I feel all right now."

Sam said, "Be careful, Tag. Don't try to do too much all at once."

Tag grinned at him. That was a laugh. He had to take on Quinlan and Leach and Romolo and Sierra and maybe he'd have to take Miles on too. But he wasn't to do too much. He went out, blinking in the sunlight, feeling the pain knife through his head from the glare. He didn't know where to start looking for Miles but he wanted to find his brother first if possible. He wanted to know how much Miles knew and why Miles had attacked him without warning from behind.

Where would Miles go, he wondered. Where? He frowned, trying to make his mind work logically. Miles had struck him from behind. There had to have been a reason for his doing so. He remembered that he'd been talking to Sam Leonard just before Miles slugged him with his gun. But what had he been talking to Sam about?

His frown deepened as he tried to think. Then suddenly the frown disappeared. He remembered now. He'd been asking Sam Leonard about Quinlan and his friends and Sam had said they were probably at the hotel.

Those words must have been heard by Miles — his inquiry and Sam's reply. Then Miles had probably gone to the hotel. He'd gone to talk to Quinlan and the others, to try and find out what was going on. Or to revenge himself for the bullet wound he'd received at Canyon Creek.

He hurried toward the hotel, wincing with every step he took. Damn it, he wasn't in any shape to take on Quinlan and his crew. He wasn't even in shape to take on Miles. But he had to try.

He went into the hotel, grateful for its dimness, grateful that it was cool. He crossed the tile-floored lobby to the desk.

Larry High glanced up at him and grinned. "Lookin' for Miles, Tag?"

"Yeah. Have you seen him lately?"

"Sure. He's in the Tivoli." High gestured toward the door with a toss of his head. "He was asking about those four hardcases . . ." High glanced uneasily toward the street door as he said that, and then went on. ". . . I gave their room number to him. He went up to see them and when he came down he went into the Tivoli next door."

"What about Quinlan and his friends?"

"Right after Miles came down, Mr. Leach came down. He'd hardly gone out when the two Quinlan calls Romolo and Sierra came down. Quinlan came down last."

Tag nodded carefully, favoring his aching head. "Thanks, Larry."

"Sure."

Tag turned and headed for the door leading to the Tivoli Saloon. He felt jubilant. So far, things seemed to be favoring him. Miles was alone, just through that door in the Tivoli saloon. Quinlan and the other three were split up. Leach was alone and so was Quinlan. At least he wasn't going to have to go up against the four all at once.

He stopped in the lobby doorway leading to the saloon. He glanced around and almost immediately saw Miles sitting at a corner table at the rear. Miles was staring at the whiskey glass in his hand. There was a bottle in front of him but from here Tag couldn't tell if it was empty or full.

He crossed the room slowly. He was prepared for almost anything. Miles might come up out of his chair with his gun in his hand for all Tag knew. Or he might come roaring at Tag, swinging his fists or a chair. He stopped at Miles's table and stood looking down.

Miles glanced up. Instantly a scowl came across his face. His eyes blazed with hatred. "So it's you. I guess I didn't slug you hard enough."

Tag stared down at him. Miles was very drunk. He was drunker than Tag had ever seen him. He doubted if Miles could even stand. He switched his glance to the bottle in front of Miles and saw that it was nearly empty. Miles picked it up and dumped what was left into his glass. He picked up the glass, gulped its contents, then slammed it down. "What the hell do you want with me?"

"Just talk. Why'd you slug me anyway?"

Miles chuckled nastily. "You needed it, that's why. And maybe I'll do it again." He picked the bottle up threateningly by its neck. Tag seized it and twisted it away from him. Miles began to curse, savagely and monotonously. Tag repeated, "Why?"

"I wanted to talk to your friends, that's why. I wanted to find out what they had on you."

Tag tried not to look worried or scared. "And did you find out?"

Miles's glance shifted to the table top. He snarled, "I found out everything I wanted to know. I found out that you let them take those cattle down on Canyon Creek. I found out that they want more — a hell of a lot more than a little bunch of stock."

"Why would they tell you that? What did you promise them?"

Miles kept his glance on the table top. "I didn't promise 'em anything. Not a goddam thing."

Tag reached across the table and seized the front of his brother's shirt. He yanked Miles close to him. "Damn you, don't lie to me! What kind of deal did you make with them?"

"No deal. No deal, I tell you!" Miles literally screeched the last few words.

Tag yelled, "Where are they now? Miles, I'll kill you if you don't speak up!"

Miles slumped suddenly, a dead weight against Taggart's grasp. Tag yanked him upright again and slapped him savagely on the side of the face. "Damn you Miles, don't you pass out now!"

Miles began to mutter incoherently but he remained limp. He began to drool.

Tag stared down at him disgustedly. He knew his brother. He knew Miles pretty well. Miles wasn't a drinking man. He'd been drinking lately but he'd never been like this before. Something must have happened — something to make him deliberately and determinedly drink himself into unconsciousness today.

Furthermore, he had an idea what it was. Miles had talked to Quinlan and Leach and the other two. He'd found something out.

Had they told him about the Kansas bank robbery in which the bank guard had been shot? Had they told him about blackmailing Tag? Had they admitted stealing Circle L cattle down at Canyon Creek and shooting Miles when he interfered?

He glanced at the bartender, now staring at him with widened eyes. He said harshly, "Get me a bucket of cold water and get it fast."

"Yes, sir." The bartender scurried from behind the bar and disappeared through a door at the rear of the saloon. Tag could hear the squeak of a pump handle through the partially open door.

After several minutes, the bartender returned, carrying the bucket Tag had told him to fetch. Tag took it from him. He held it over Miles's head and began to pour — slowly — letting the stream fall squarely on the top of Miles's head.

Miles stirred, trying to get away. He began to grumble drunkenly. He raised up and batted at Tag with one arm, but Tag avoided it easily. He was thinking he ought to pour some of this water on top of his own head, which still ached terribly.

He stopped pouring water for a moment. The bartender now came to the table carrying a mop and another bucket. Scowling, he began to mop up the water from the floor.

Tag dumped the rest of the water over Miles. His brother was now thoroughly soaked. He reared back in his chair and began to curse Tag angrily.

Tag put the bucket down. He leaned across the table and slapped Miles's face, back and forth, back and forth, a dozen times. Miles tried to get his gun out but Tag twisted it away from him and threw it across the room. He roared, "You sonofabitch, talk!"

Miles was shivering violently, partly from cold, partly from fear, partly from the furious intensity of his hate. He kept cursing steadily.

Tag shouted, "Where are they? What kind of deal did you make with them?"

Miles stared at him and for an instant — for the briefest kind of instant — there was sanity in his eyes. Sanity and hatred greater than any Tag had ever seen before. Then Miles began to laugh, harshly, drunkenly. "What kind of deal? I cut them in on Circle L, that's what I did. I cut them in if they'd cut you out. What do you think of that, you lousy bastard? What do you think of that?"

"Cut them in? How the hell could you cut them in? You don't own anything at Circle L. No more than I own anything."

Miles continued to chuckle. "Mebbe not, but I will and you won't. Because you'll be dead. You'll be dead an' . . ." He stopped suddenly.

Tag slapped the side of his face. He was raging now and he knew he was running out of time. He had forgotten the awful pain in his head. He had forgotten everything but his sudden, terrible feeling of urgency. He roared, "What are they going to do? I'll be dead and what?"

"So will the old man."

Tag stared at Miles, horror in his eyes. Miles had made a deal with them all right, a deal for them to kill his own father and brother in return for a part of the monstrous, wealthy ranch.

But he wasted little time in disgust for Miles. He was already on his way to the door. Somehow he had to reach home before Quinlan got there. Somehow he had to get there in time to save his father's life.

CHAPTER THIRTEEN

Taggart burst through the swinging doors of the Tivoli Saloon. The bright sunlight momentarily blinded him and made spots dance before his eyes. He staggered, steadied himself on the wall of the saloon, hanging there for a moment as though too drunk to stand.

His head reeled crazily. The street seemed to tip, only gradually righting itself. Tag shook his head angrily. He hadn't time for weakness now; he hadn't time for dizziness. He had to reach his horse and get on out to the ranch. He had to do it fast.

His horse was still tied down in front of the Buckhorn. He started that way, fighting his weakness and dizziness, trying to force his head to clear by the power of his will.

It seemed like a mile to where his horse was tied, the sun getting brighter and hotter all the time. The blow Miles had struck him on the head must have done more damage than he had thought. The sheriff had been right. He shouldn't try to do this by himself. He ought to ask for help.

Then he thought of all the questions Lew Wintergill would ask. He realized how impossible it would be to keep the truth from the sheriff once he told him part of it. And he shook his head imperceptibly. There was nothing Wintergill could do that he couldn't do. There was no need for the law out at Circle L. All that was needed there was a loaded gun and a man holding it who knew how deadly and unscrupulous Quinlan and Leach could be. Tag knew, and Tag would not hesitate to shoot to kill. Lew Wintergill didn't know and he'd probably try to arrest the pair so that they could be brought to trial. As well try to arrest an infuriated grizzly bear. All Quinlan and Leach would understand today was lead.

He was halfway there now — halfway to his horse. Farther down the street the door of the Pink Lady Saloon opened and a man came out.

Tag recognized the man instantly in spite of the distance separating them. He would recognize that slight form anywhere. It was the Mexican, the one called Sierra, the one who smiled and smiled, but who could throw his knife with such deadly accuracy.

The distance to Tag's horse was about the same for Tag as it was for the Mexican. Tag began to hurry. He cursed the dizziness that threatened to overcome him. He fought the way things reeled before his eyes. How could he fight Sierra and win when he could scarcely see the man?

Furthermore, he knew from experience that, wherever Sierra was, there also was Romolo. The two were never separated. If Sierra was here in the street of Landry, then Romolo was also here.

He glanced behind him uneasily, glanced to right and left, trying to search each doorway, each passageway, each vacant lot. Romolo was as deadly with his gun as Sierra was with his knife.

Romolo and Sierra here. Quinlan and Leach out at the home place. And he understood the plan, the plan Miles had set in motion before he retreated into drunkenness. Quinlan and Leach were supposed to get rid of the old man — by telling him the truth about his son, and if that didn't work by using whatever other means were necessary.

Romolo and Sierra had stayed here in town. They had been hunting him even while he hunted them. Except that Tag was now at a terrible disadvantage. Miles had seen to that. Tag could scarcely walk, could scarcely stand. How could he fight this deadly pair and win?

He'd have to get the sheriff's help. He had no other choice. Whatever happened to him, they must not be allowed to kill the old man.

Fighting desperately to keep from staggering, Tag began to run. And Sierra released a sudden shout as he also began to run.

Lew Wintergill's office seemed a thousand miles away. Sierra was closer to it than he. Sierra would pass it and meet him before he even had a chance to yell out for Lew Wintergill.

But his horse was closer . . . his horse was tied in front of the Buckhorn Saloon. If he could reach his horse . . . and he could . . . he could mount and avoid Sierra and his deadly knife. He could reach Lew Wintergill's place by a roundabout way, or even by way of the alley at the rear, if Romolo didn't show up and interfere. The range of Sierra's knife was something less than a hundred feet. Romolo's gun would be accurate at twice that distance or more.

The horse heard him coming and turned his head. His eyes rolled with sudden fright, showing Tag their whites. The frightened animal pulled back against the reins, which Tag had looped around the tie rail in front of the saloon.

Tag forced himself to stop. He had to force himself, one eye on the horse, one on Sierra, coming on at his doglike lope, knife already in his hand. Sierra . . . with his long, straight hair, his dark-skinned face, his everlasting smile that seemed to have something so unclean to it. Tag spoke soothingly to the horse, approaching the animal from a distance of forty feet at a walk. He was hoping the horse would not pull free and move away, move even closer to Sierra than he was right now.

It was going to be close, he thought. Oh God, it would be close. He lunged the last ten fet and seized the horse's reins. He literally yanked them from the tie rail, turning the horse, keeping the horse's body between himself and Sierra's deadly knife.

He swung to the saddle, digging spurs, whirling the horse and pointing him up the street. He saw Romolo come from another saloon across the street from the hotel the instant the horse surged into motion up the street.

Reins in his left hand, he now drew his revolver with his right. He thumbed the hammer back, holding the gun loosely, almost negligently in his hand.

Sudden movement had sent blood pounding to his head. Now it dizzied him so that he reeled in the saddle and nearly toppled out of it. He grabbed the saddle horn with his left hand and held on so that he would not fall.

Romolo was running toward him, gun in hand. Romolo was now halfway across the street, coming diagonally along it toward him . . . Damn it, why couldn't he see the man clearly? Why did Romolo's running form have to be so blurred? Why did the man's body separate, until it was two men running, or seemed to be?

He closed one eye and the double vision disappeared. He closed the other eye and the form shifted slightly to the right.

Oh God, which one was he supposed to shoot at? Which one? He couldn't afford to miss. If he missed with his first shot he'd be dead. He'd not get a second chance.

The decision was taken suddenly out of his hands. Romolo fired, a quick, off-hand shot released without even slowing down or breaking stride.

It was not surprising that it missed. At a range of nearly a hundred yards, running, not even Romolo's deadly accuracy was of much use. But the bullet stung Taggart's horse. It creased his neck, low and in front, and because it stung it immediately brought him to a plunging halt and started him bucking savagely.

Tag had time only to jamb the gun back into its holster. Then he was holding on for life, holding to the saddle horn, trying to keep his head from being whipped back and forth with every jump the horse took, trying desperately to hang onto his consciousness.

Romolo stopped now, waiting calmly, gun in hand, for the horse to stop, or come close enough so that he could shoot with some certainty of hitting his target.

Grimly Tag fought his bucking horse. He was angry now, angry because everything seemed suddenly to be conspiring against him. He yanked up on the reins so savagely he nearly broke the leather, but he brought the horse's head up; he straightened the bowed neck and he brought the horse to a plunging halt.

Romolo raised his gun and took careful aim. Sierra, now almost close enough, drew back his hand to throw.

Tag was almost blind with pain. The sun seemed a thousand times brighter than it ever had before. He could scarcely see Romolo but he could see enough to know the man was steadying his gun to shoot.

And Sierra — Sierra was down the street, smiling, coming on, almost caressing the gleaming blade he balanced so lightly in his hand. Suddenly Tag wanted Sierra more than he had ever wanted anything. He wanted to erase that deadly, unclean smile. He wanted to stop that murderous knife forever so that it could never take another life.

Furiously, he sank spurs into his lathered horse's sides. He yanked the horse around and pointed him straight at the long-haired little Mexican with the gleaming knife.

Already terrified with fear, the horse bellied down to the ground and ran. In split seconds he covered the distance separating him from the little man with the knife. Unerringly he headed for Sierra, straightened by Tag's hand on the reins every time he tried to veer aside.

For once, Sierra let himself be rushed. The sight of Tag's contorted face above that horse approaching him with such speed forced him to step aside, forced him to fling the knife with less than his customary care.

It whirled through the air, catching the sun and throwing it flashing back as it turned over and over on its way to Tag.

Like a branding iron it raked Tag's thigh, cutting through his trouser leg, cutting his long thigh muscles with its razor-sharp edge. Then it was past, and Tag was literally on top of Sierra, who now dived aside in panic.

But Tag wouldn't let him escape. Tag's gun was in his hand again. His left hand held the reins, forcing the terrified horse to do exactly as he wished. The horse struck Sierra with a shoulder. A hind foot caught the deadly knife-fighter as the horse flashed past. Sierra went down, and rolled, raising a cloud from the dusty street.

Tag whirled the horse so abruptly the animal reared, fighting for the bit. On his back in the dusty street, Sierra now drew the small gun he carried in his belt, the short-range derringer that had two barrels and two shots.

Tag was immediately over him as he raised the gun to shoot. And Tag pointed his own gun at Sierra, aiming the gun straight at the man's smiling face and squeezed off his shot.

Tag's gun and Sierra's fired so closely, one sounded like an echo of the other. But the loudest had been first. Tag had fired first.

Sierra was driven back, driven literally into the dust of the street. He was slammed back, flat. His arms flew out wide and the gun flew out of his hand.

A tiny trickle of blood ran from between the Mexican's eyes. But he did not move. There was no rise and fall to Sierra's chest. The knife lay harmlessly, its blade red with Taggart's blood, thirty feet away where he had thrown it only moments before.

The door of the sheriff's office slammed open and Lew Wintergill came charging out. He bawled, "What the hell . . . ?"

Tag looked down at his thigh, now streaming blood. He felt sick at his stomach, but he couldn't have said whether killing Sierra had caused it or whether it was caused by the sight of so much of his own blood. Certainly he had no reason to regret taking Sierra's life. If ever a killing had been in self-defense, this one had. But it wasn't over. There still was Romolo, more deadly in his own way than Sierra could ever be.

He raised his glance and stared up the street. Romolo was still there, but he had stopped. He had his eyes on the sheriff. The odds had changed suddenly. Before it had been he and Sierra against Tag, two to one. Now the same odds were reversed.

Romolo decided he didn't like the odds. Slamming his revolver back into its holster at his side, he turned and bolted.

The sheriff roared, "Hold it! Halt, or I'll shoot!"

Romolo didn't stop. Lew Wintergill fired a shot but it was fired into the air in the hopes of stopping the fleeing man. It didn't work. Romolo disappeared into a passageway between Sartoris's Gun Shop and the Landry Hardware Store.

His thigh streaming blood, Tag sat his horse in the middle of the street. Lew Wintergill, gun in hand, ran past him with only a swift upward glance. He saw the blood and shouted back. "Get into the Buckhorn, Tag. Sam can take care of that." Then he was gone, and an instant later he charged into the passageway where Romolo had disappeared only seconds earlier.

For a moment Tag stared at Sierra's body, so small and insignificant in death. He hadn't time to wait for his leg to be patched up. He hadn't time for anything. Quinlan and Leach had a good head start on him as it was. They could be halfway to the ranch.

People were streaming out into the street — curious people, who would want to aid him but who would only delay him with their questions and their offers to help. A man shouted. "Hey, Tag, what's goin' on? You need some help?" but Tag did not reply.

The man ran to Sierra's body and stood looking down at him. Others gathered, more cautiously, standing back as though afraid the gunplay might start again.

Tag whirled his horse and sank spurs into the animal's sweaty sides. He pounded down the street, heading toward the ranch. Wintergill would follow as soon as he could, he realized. But he couldn't wait for Wintergill. He couldn't wait for anything.

He cleared the town, holding onto the saddle horn, gritting his teeth against the pain in his head and thigh, against the nausea threatening to overcome him. He didn't know if he'd be any good when he did arrive at the ranch, but if he didn't try, if he didn't give it his very best he'd never be able to live with himself again.

One thing he knew; if Quinlan and Leach injured his father in any way, they'd never live to benefit from whatever share Miles had promised them in the ranch. Tag would kill them, in any way he could, no matter how long it took.

No longer did it matter — the Kansas Bank robbery and the penalty for the shooting of the guard. Those things which had seemed so important to Tag now faded into relative insignificance. He was fighting for survival now, for his own survival and for his father's life. If he saved his father's life and survived himself he knew he would turn himself in and admit his part in the crime two years ago. He'd take his punishment.

It was a long ride out to the ranch. Today would be the longest ride Tag had ever made. He was a mile from town when he heard a rifle shot behind. He turned his head to look.

A horseman was leaving town, pounding toward him along the dusty road. A man stood at the edge of town, rifle in his hands. Even as Tag watched, a puff of smoke issued from the muzzle of the rifle.

The rider did not slow down. Leaning low over his horse's withers he came on, spurring the horse. And Tag knew who it was. It was Romolo.

He was sick and near collapse. He had two killers ahead of him and one behind. He didn't see how he possibly could win. But he gritted his teeth angrily and dug his spurs deeply into his running horse's sides.

CHAPTER FOURTEEN

There was time on that long ride out to the ranch buildings to think, and time for bitter regret over past mistakes. It had been a mistake to leave here in the first place two years ago. The reasons for his leaving had been wrong. Even if he had been right in believing Miles was his father's favorite, it should not have been cause for him to leave. He had acted like a spoiled kid.

Getting himself involved with Quinlan and Leach and the other two had been the second mistake, even worse than the first had been, but the motive behind his doing so had been the same. Again he had acted like a kid.

Only when he had separated from the other four, only when he had gotten an honest job, only when he had stuck to it and worked hard at it had he really begun to behave like a man. He guessed there was no way people could avoid paying for their mistakes. He was paying for his now, Tag's father was paying and Miles was paying too.

He glanced behind often, and dug spurs into his horse's sides. He was maintaining the mile lead he had over Romolo. But a mile was not enough. He had to increase that lead if he possibly could. He had to have time to tangle with Quinlan and Leach before Romolo arrived. Fighting two at once would be bad enough. Fighting three would be impossible.

But he could not increase the lead, no matter how he tried. He was killing his horse maintaining it.

Now his vision began to blur again and his head started to ache almost intolerably. Damn Miles for hitting him so hard!

Several times he caught himself dozing in the saddle, yet he knew it was not really dozing. He was close to passing out, close to unconsciousness.

There was no need to guess what would happen if he did pass out. He'd fall from the saddle. He'd never regain consciousness. Romolo, coming along behind, would simply club him on the head again in the same place Miles had hit him earlier. It would be made to order for the four outlaws. He would be dead and Miles would stand trial for killing him. No one would know it had not been Miles's blow that caused his death.

And out at the ranch, Quinlan and Leach would see to it that the old man died. One way or another, they'd see to that.

He didn't quite understand how they'd get their hands on Circle L. He supposed they'd get control of it through Miles, by promising to break him out of jail. He'd be desperate enough to agree to anything.

How they'd get Circle L didn't matter right now anyway. All that mattered at this moment was his father's life. His horse's sides were bloody from the spurs. His neck was flecked with foam. He was wheezing hard and Tag knew he couldn't last much longer at this pace.

Behind him, Romolo's horse was better off. Romolo's mount was fresh while Tag's had made an earlier ride into town. But he didn't dare let up. He'd be no worse off if the horse dropped dead than he would if he slowed the animal. Romolo would catch him either way.

There was another alternative that he considered briefly. He could stop and have it out with Romolo right now. Afterward, if he was still alive, he could take Romolo's horse and go on.

There was only one thing wrong with that. It would take up too much time. Emmett Landry's life might depend on a minute or maybe less. He shook his head and gouged his horse again mercilessly with the spurs.

At last, after what seemed an eternity, he saw the ranch buildings ahead of him. Immediately he tried to force his horse to an even faster pace, for behind him Romolo was beginning slowly to gain on him. He shook his head in a futile effort to clear it, to improve his vision and throw off the deadly feeling of drowsiness creeping over him.

Raising a cloud of dust now, his horse pounded down the slight slope toward the huge cluster of buildings dominated by the house. Tag thundered into the yard, seeing the two horses tied to the rail at the kitchen door, seeing the empty rocking chair on the long front porch.

He shot a glance toward the bunkhouse, then swept the yard with his stare. There were a few horses in the corral. There were a dozen white chickens scratching in the dry dust in front of the barn. But otherwise the place was deserted — except for the old man and Quinlan and Leach inside, except for Wong, who never left the ranch and who might be already dead.

The back door slammed open as Tag thundered up to it. Leach stood there, gun in hand, trying to bring it to bear on Tag but waiting, waiting until he could be sure of his shot.

Tag stayed in his saddle as the horse plunged to a halt, riding out the rough jolts with gun in hand, also waiting until the horse would be still enough for him to shoot.

Dust rolled over him in a cloud. But it was not thick enough to obscure Leach or to keep Tag from firing an instant before Leach did.

His bullet struck — hard enough to spin Leach around, hard enough to spoil his shot but not hard enough to put him down. He ducked back inside the house, leaving Tag exposed with nothing at which to shoot. He shot a glance over his shoulder at Romolo, approaching fast. Damn it, if he only had a little time! If he only had more time!

He left his saddle at the same instant a rifle fired inside the kitchen door. Striking the horse, the bullet made a loud sound, almost like that of a bullet striking water. The horse pitched to his knees. He stayed that way for an instant before going all the way down. Blood ran from his nostrils and his mouth. But Tag only noticed it with part of his mind. He was trapped, pinned here behind his horse. Whoever had fired the rifle inside the house was waiting now for his second shot, waiting until Tag would expose himself.

The corner of the house seemed a thousand miles away. Already Tag could hear the rapid pound of hoofs, the hoofs of Romolo's approaching horse. He glanced up frantically. Romolo was less than a quarter of a mile away. Tag's time had run out. He pulled his hands and knees under him. With a burst of effort he leaped to his feet and plunged toward the corner of the house.

Instantly the rifle boomed inside the house. Smoke billowed out the open door. The bullet whined viciously as it passed. It tugged at a loose fold of Tag's shirt as he ran.

But he was clear and there was now no time for his assailant to lever a new shell into the gun and fire again before he disappeared. He heard a savage, disappointed curse inside the house.

He was behind the corner, head pounding savagely, reeling as he tried to stop and regain his balance and turn to face Romolo, now approaching.

He had not changed the odds, he thought bitterly. He had gained only a temporary respite, not a lasting one. He still had three men to face and beat. He was still just one gun against their three.

He must make a choice, he realized. He must either stay here and try to get Romolo as he rode into the yard, or he must circle the house and try to gain entry to it before the two inside anticipated his plan and moved to intercept him, to shoot him down as he came in.

He chose to try and get into the house. His father's safety was all-important. Now that he was here, both Quinlan and Leach would try to get rid of the old man as quickly as they could.

He turned and ran again, nearly stumbling over the slanting door to the cellar his father had dug beneath the house years ago when it was built. He bent, and raised it, and ducked down the moldy-smelling stairs. No one had been down in this cellar for years. It had been put here originally as protection in case of Indian attack and the outside entrance had been added later for convenience. Now it would either save Taggart Landry's life or be his tomb.

Halfway down the stairs, he reached up and closed the door above his head. Almost instantly he heard the pound of a horse's hoofs as the animal came to a plunging halt but a dozen feet away. He heard Romolo's disappointed shout, "He ain't here! The sonofabitch is gone!"

He remembered the cellar from the times he had played in it as a boy. Cobwebs brushed his face. The stale, moldy air filled his nostrils and his lungs. There was a stairway going up into the kitchen, but he decided now that he didn't dare use that. Not with both Quinlan and Leach waiting for him at the head of the stairs. They creaked and would give his presence away.

But there was another way. There was a narrow passageway dug out from the front of the house. It emerged fifty feet away in the middle of a thick clump of willows planted to screen it twenty-five years before. If he could crawl along that passageway he could emerge where they would least expect him to be. He might get a chance to pick one or two of them off before he could be seen.

He entered the passageway. He could smell the rotting timbers that kept the floors from caving in. He brushed away the cobwebs irritably from his face. He had to crawl here and he was frantic now with worry for his father. He had to get inside the house, no matter what, he had to get inside.

Reaching the end of the passageway, he clawed his way up through the tangle of willows that had grown over the entrance to it. He raised his head and could see the house. He could see Romolo, sitting on his horse beside the front porch looking around puzzledly. And he saw Leach, a bloody spot on the shoulder of his shirt, standing there with Romolo.

Leach said, "He couldn't have just disappeared. He must've . . ."

Tag suddenly knew what he was going to do. He raised his gun, sighted carefully on Romolo and fired instantly. Before he saw whether the bullet had hit or not, he changed his point of aim and fired again at Leach.

Romolo's horse began to buck, dumping the gunman on his second jump. Romolo fell to the ground, doubling, clutching his thigh and yelling, "The sonofabitch got me, Leach!"

"Well anyway we know where he is! Come on!"

Leach came across the yard at a crouching run. Romolo limped after him, gun ready in his hand. Tag fired again, but this time his bullet ticked the willows as it left the barrel of his gun and it sang away into space.

It had served its purpose, though. It forced both Leach and Romolo to drop flat on the ground where they were hidden by the grass and weeds.

Without hesitation, Tag now withdrew and retraced his way along the passageway. He was moving as fast as he possibly could, feeling ahead of his face as he moved along, careful to make no unnecessary noise. Leach and Romolo would be immobilized for five minutes at the very least while they stalked the clump of willows in search of him. By the time they discovered the passageway he should be inside the house where Quinlan was.

He reached the basement proper and charged across it to the foot of the kitchen stairs. He plunged up the stairs, striking the door with his shoulder with every bit of strength he possessed.

The impact stopped him in his tracks with a shock that nearly robbed him of consciousness. But he had heard a splintering sound and now reared back and hit the door again.

This time it gave with a crash, dumping him flat on top of it on the kitchen floor. He was close to unconsciousness, closer than he had been since he regained it hours before in the Buckhorn saloon. Brilliant spots swam before his eyes. There was a brassy taste in his mouth.

It took a monstrous effort of will, but he forced himself to move and move fast. He rolled off the door as a bullet ripped it where he had been. He rolled behind the table, momentarily shielded by it from Quinlan, who stood in the center of the room, a smoking revolver in his hand.

His body hit Wong, unconscious on the floor, a butcher knife in his hand.

Recklessly, Quinlan put a bullet through the table on the chance that it might hit Tag. It did not. It buried itself in the floor six inches from his face, showering him with splinters from the floor.

He still had not seen his father, but he had seen very little crashing into the room. He had glimpsed Quinlan merely as a shape as he rolled behind the table a few seconds earlier. He had encountered Wong because Wong was here unconscious on the floor.

Gun in hand, he stared across the room at knee level, and now saw exactly where Quinlan was. Spread-legged the man stood, leaning forward, his stance tense. He was like a cat tensed just outside a rat's hole waiting for the rat to reappear.

Tag knew he could smash one of Quinlan's legs. He also knew he wanted more than that. Carefully, moving silently, Tag got to his hands and knees. He moved back, so that when he raised up he would clear the table doing so.

He knew the risk he took. Quinlan was ready. Quinlan could get off a shot a full second before he could. He was a fool to take such a chance. A fool . . .

He changed his mind about standing because he suddenly knew how he could even the odds, with Quinlan at least. He raised his revolver and took careful aim on one of Quinlan's legs just above the knee. If he couldn't raise himself to Quinlan's level and stay alive, he could bring Quinlan down to his.

The bullet struck, dumping Quinlan to the floor by taking the legs out from under him. Apparently there was, for the moment, no sensation of pain, no realization of what had actually happened to him. Quinlan stayed conscious and in full possession of his faculties. As he struck the floor the first thing he did was to bring his gun to bear on Tag.

Tag fired an instant before Quinlan did, an instant, but not soon enough to wholly deflect Quinlan's aim. The bullet seared along his ribs, feeling like a red-hot branding iron but leaving a feeling of warm wetness in its wake.

Tag's bullet struck Quinlan squarely in the throat, severing the jugular vein, bringing an instant flood of blood. Choking on his own blood, Quinlan fell face downward on the floor. Tag stared at him unbelievingly for an instant before he moved.

He heard a sound and, rising, turned his head toward it. Emmett Landry sat in a chair on the far side of the room. His face was red and congested with blood. His hands shook violently bearing down on the arms of his chair as he tried to rise.

Tag said, "Easy Pa. It's all right now. Now I've got a chance."

The old man sank back, relaxing his hands on the arms of the chair. His lips moved and his words came out in a hoarse whisper. "A gun. Give me a gun."

Tag didn't have time to answer him. He heard the other two, Leach and Romolo, approaching the kitchen door, their boots pounding as they ran. He was pushing fresh shells into his empty gun with fingers that trembled violently. But he got in three before he ran out of time.

CHAPTER FIFTEEN

Leach burst through the door first, his glance switching from Quinlan's body on the floor to the old man and then to Tag. His gun swiveled with his glance, firing the instant it was in line.

But Tag was moving too, moving away from the center of the room, moving fast because he understood that Leach had burst through quickly so that Romolo could enter immediately behind.

Smoke billowed out from the muzzle of Leach's gun. The bullet thudded into the wall. Tag caught movement across the room where his father was but didn't dare look that way. Not now. Not with Romolo surely right behind Leach, with Leach following him with his gun and ready to shoot again.

He slammed into a chair and fell over it as Leach's gun flared a second time. The second bullet cut through the air where he would have been had it not been for the chair.

He was down on the floor, sprawled out, but he brought his gun to bear and fired, taking only hasty aim at Leach.

The man gave a monstrous grunt as the bullet struck, and straightened, stiffening. He stood that way an instant and Tag fired at him again as a corner of his vision caught the movement of Romolo coming through the door.

Romolo did not come in as Leach had done. His gun and arm came in first and then just enough of him so that he could see where to shoot.

Tag's gun bucked against his palm. The instant it did he knew he had fired too hastily and he knew something else that turned him cold all the way to the bottom of his spine. His gun was empty now. He'd only had time to punch three shells into it and now all three were gone.

He'd missed Romolo cleanly with that last hasty shot. And now he'd die for his one small mistake. He'd almost defeated the four and had killed three of them but he'd die and his father would die because he'd made that one small mistake. As though he knew the gun was empty, Romolo now stepped into the room.

Suddenly Tag's anger was towering. He was, in this instant, more furious than he had ever been in his life before. He'd all but done the impossible and to be cheated of his success this way . . .

Standing, facing Romolo, he flung his gun the way he might have flung a rock.

Turning over and over in the air, it struck Rolomo squarely in the chest. It made a sound as it struck, a sodden, dull sound, and it drove a gust of air from Romolo like the one the bullet had earlier driven from Leach. But it didn't kill the murder in Romolo's eyes. It didn't stop his deadly, lifting gun. It wouldn't stop the slight pressure of his finger that would send the bullet on its way.

Tag knew he was beaten. He was finished. In the split part of another second he would be dead. He straightened, and glared, and waited for death to come.

A gun roared and the room filled suddenly with powder-smoke, but no bullet struck Tag. Instead, Romolo was driven toward him as though cuffed by some gigantic hand. He collapsed, falling face downward at Taggart's feet.

Across the body of Romolo, through the swirling smoke, he saw his father standing over Leach, holding Leach's smoking gun in his hand. And once again this was the man he remembered from so long ago. His father's eyes were narrowed and they blazed with rage. His father's face was flushed, but his hand was steady as a rock.

Tag suddenly felt weak. His head whirled and for a moment he felt as though he was going to fall. He put out a hand and steadied himself against the wall. His father said, "Now by God that it's over, maybe you'll get around to telling me what it's all about."

Tag grinned faintly at him. "I guess if you can take this, you can take anything I've got to say."

The old man nodded angrily. "I expect I can."

Sudden, new sound filled the room, the sound of many hoofs pounding into the yard outside. The old man crossed to the door, his smoking gun still in his hand, and stepped outside. Tag followed him, feeling sheepish in the face of his father's anger at him.

Lew Wintergill and half a dozen others were pulling their plunging horses to a halt outside. Wintergill got down and came immediately to Tag and his father on the porch. When Tag said, "It's all over sheriff," he turned his head and nodded to the men with him and they rode their horses across the yard to the water trough just outside the corral. Tag said, "I guess you'd better both hear this because you're both concerned. Quinlan was blackmailing me because two years ago I rode with them when they robbed a Kansas bank. A guard was shot — Quinlan shot him — and we got away. We split up and were going to meet and split the loot down in the Nations. But I didn't go down to the Nations for my share. I didn't see them again until they came here."

Wintergill stared closely at him, a frown of concentration on his face. "Where in Kansas? Hays?"

Tag nodded. "How did you know?"

Lew grinned humorlessly. "Banks don't get robbed every day. That was the only bank robbery in Kansas two years ago." He studied Tag's face carefully. "The bank guard didn't die. He's fully recovered. My guess would be that if you'd make restitution for the amount stolen there'd be no charge. Particularly in view of what's happened here today."

Tag stared at the sheriff in disbelief. He felt like an utter fool. He'd been fighting and struggling to conceal his part in the Kansas crime. He'd paid blackmail and would have gone on paying indefinitely if only the blackmail had been reasonable. And all for nothing. If he'd gone to Lew Wintergill in the first place and told him the truth all this could have been avoided. The law would have been helping him, not hindering.

He said, "Miles . . ."

Wintergill looked at the old man. "Miles slugged Tag back in town with the barrel of his gun. For a while I thought he'd killed him but I guess Tag's too hard-headed for that. But he ought to be in bed."

The old man nodded. Tag's head was splitting with pain but he couldn't take his eyes from his father's face. There was a suspicious shine to the old man's eyes as he said, "I never told you this, Tag, because it didn't seem important at the time. Now I guess it is. Miles isn't your brother. He's an orphan I found in a wagon out on the plain when he was just a little boy. He was alone and I took him in to raise."

Tag stared. This explained so many things. It explained Miles's hatred of him. It explained how Miles could nearly kill him by slugging him from behind. It explained how Miles could plot his death and the old man's death with Quinlan and the rest. He said, "What about Miles, Pa?"

The old man smiled faintly. "I guess he needs a family now more than he ever did."

Tag stared closely at his father's face. He said, "I was pretty stupid, going away like that. But I'll stay here now. I'll stay as long as you'll let me stay."

Emmett Landry nodded. There were tears in his eyes and no further need for words.

The old man's illness, the failure of his heart — these things had been real enough. But he'd have recovered completely long before now if he hadn't lost the will to try. Now he had the will to try again. His son was home.

Lew Wintergill said harshly, "I'll need the loan of a wagon, Mr. Landry, to take these bodies back to town."

Emmett Landry said, "Help yourself, Lew. Help yourself." He had hold of Tag's arm and was helping him into the house. And he was grinning, really grinning, for the first time since Tag's return.

Lewis B. Patten wrote more than ninety Western novels in thirty years and three of them won Spur Awards from the Western Writers of America and the author himself the Golden Saddleman Award. Indeed, this highlights the most remarkable aspect of his work: not that there is so much of it, but that so much of it is so fine. Patten was born in Denver, Colorado, and served in the U.S. Navy 1933–1937. He was educated at the University of Denver during the war years and became an auditor for the Colorado Department of Revenue during the 1940s. It was in this period that he began contributing significantly to Western pulp magazines, fiction that was from the beginning fresh and unique and revealed Patten's lifelong concern with the sociological and psychological affects of group psychology on the frontier. He became a professional writer at the time of his first novel, *Massacre at White River* (1952). The dominant theme in much of his fiction is the notion of justice, and its opposite, injustice. In his first novel it has to do with exploitation of the Ute Indians, but as he matured as a writer he explored this theme with significant and poignant detail in small towns throughout the early West. Crimes, such as rape or lynching, were often at the centre of his stories. When the values embodied in these small towns are examined closely, they are found to be wanting.

Conformity is always easier than taking a stand. Yet, in Patten's view of the American West, there is usually a man or a woman who refuses to conform. Among his finest titles, always a difficult choice, surely are *A Killing at Kiowa* (1972), *Ride a Crooked Trail* (1976), and his many fine contributions to Doubleday's Double D series, including *Villa's Rifles* (1977), *The Law at Cottonwood* (1978), and *Death Rides a Black Horse* (1978). His most recent books are *Tincup in the Storm Country* (1996), *Trail to Vicksburg* (1997), *Death Rides the Denver Stage* (1999), and *The Woman at Ox-Yoke* (2000).